I0589487

Also by
Christine Keleny

The Rose Series:
Rosebloom
Rose From the Ashes

Historical Fiction:
Will the Real Carolyn Keene
Please Stand Up

Memoir:
Living in the
House of Drugs

Family Books:
The Red Velvet Box
Intrigue in Istanbul:
An Agnes Kelly Mystery Adventure

A BURNISHED ROSE

Book I

A Novel by Christine Keleny

CKBooks

Publisher's Cataloging-In-Publication Data
(Prepared by The Donohue Group, Inc.)

Keleny, Christine.
  A burnished rose : a novel / by Christine Keleny.

  p. : ill., maps ; cm. -- (Rosebloom ; 2)

  Includes bibliographical references.
  ISBN: 978-0-9832984-2-7

  1. Nurses--United States--20th century--Fiction. 2. World War, 1939-1945--Medical care--Europe--Fiction. 3. World War, 1939-1945--Women--Fiction. 4. World War, 1939-1945--Hospitals--Europe--Fiction. 5. Historical fiction. 6. Bildungsromans. I. Title.

PS3611.E4464 B87 2011
813/.6

Cover art: Aaron Keleny Parks
Cover graphics and interior design: Bill Martinelli

To my father, Lloyd J. Keleny and
Marcy Schlemma/Korda and
all the other service men and women who
give their service and their lives to our county.
I can not thank you enough.

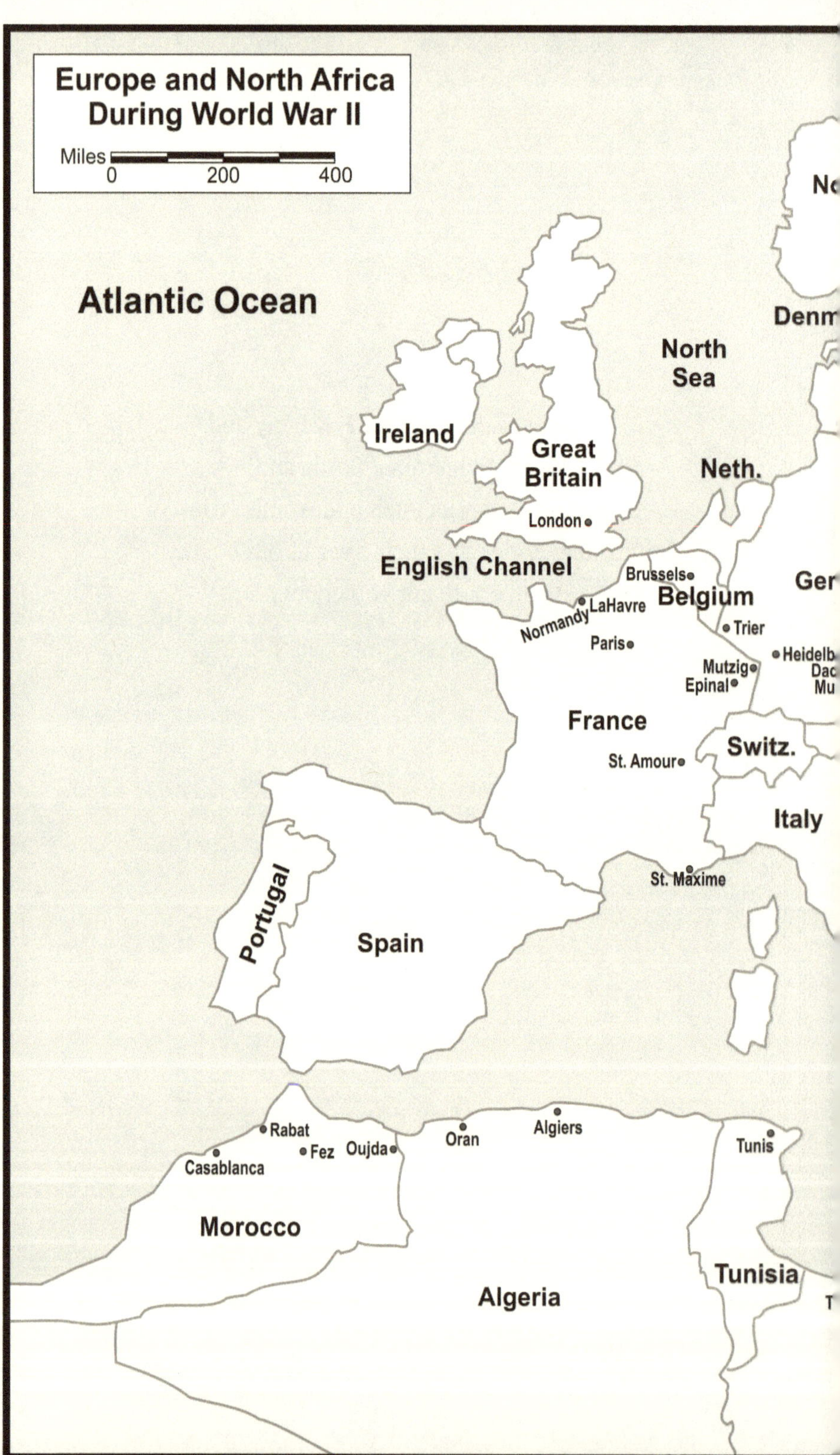

Europe and North Africa
During World War II
Miles
0
200
400
Atlantic Ocean
North
Sea
Denm
No
Ireland
Great
Britain
Neth.
London
English Channel
Brussels
Belgium
Ger
Normandy
LaHavre
Trier
Paris
Heidelb
Mutzig
Dac
Epinal
Mu
France
Switz.
St. Amour
Italy
Portugal
St. Maxime
Spain
Rabat
Algiers
Oran
Tunis
Fez
Oujda
Casablanca
Morocco
Tunisia
Algeria
T

Finland
Sweden
Copenhagen
Berlin
Warsaw
Poland
Dresden
Prague
Czech.
Salzburg
Vienna
Austria
Hungary
Yugoslavia
Romania
Bulgaria
Albania
Naples
Salerno
Greece
Moscow
Soviet Union
Stalingrad
Yalta
Black Sea
Mediterranean Sea
El Alamein
Cairo
Libya
Egypt
N

N
Mongolia
China
Korea
Hiroshima
Tok[yo]
Nagasaki
Japan
India
Hengyang
Kunming
Hong Kong
Burma
The Philippine
Islands
Rangoon
Thailand
French
Indochina
South
China
Sea
Singapore
New
Guinea
Indian
Ocean
Australia

The Pacific Theater
During World War II
Miles
0
500
1000
Midway
Oahu
Pearl Harbor
Wake Island
Guam
Pacific Ocean
Guadacanel
Coral
Sea

Book I

1

Coming Home

Rose Krantz blinked away the tears from her eyes as she stared at her mother, Lilly. Lilly stared back, green eyes soft and waiting. Rose was trying to decide where to start after her mother had asked her about her two long years away from home.

Both women were full of questions, of course, but what Lilly really wanted to know was if Rose was home to stay. Rose's mother would have to wait for her answer, however. Lilly wasn't in the same hurry as the bright-eyed seventeen-year-old sitting next to her at the kitchen table.

Actually, that same question loomed in Rose's mind as well. Rose looked at her mother and sighed.

Here is the woman who gave me life, who fed me, clothed me, watched over me when I was ill, and who almost died while I was away following my dream—a dream it seems only I think is worthwhile following—and already I'm wondering how long can I really stay.

But Rose decided she couldn't think about that now. Three weeks ago Lilly had come down with pneumonia, and it had almost cost her her life. The guilt of being gone at such a time sent Rose running back home to their farm in southwest Wisconsin.

The women were sitting together in a kitchen that floated in the sweet aroma of pancake syrup mixed with earthy, bitter coffee, remnants of the morning meal. Lilly Mae—Rose's friend—was sitting quietly next to Rose. Gertrude—Rose's older sister—was standing at the sink. Dishes were stacked high on the countertop sitting next to a sink of hot, soapy water left hastily by Gerty when she discovered who the two unexpected visitors were.

"We can talk about me later, Mom. How are *you* feeling? When did you get out of the hospital? I came home because Michael said you were in the hospital."

"You saw Michael!" Gerty blurted out.

Gerty had been listening covertly though intently for what the two women would say to each other. She anticipated some sharp words between the pair.

It wasn't as if Rose had just gone off to live with relatives for two years with the family's permission; she had run away from home. And other than a small note she had left next to the flour jar, she hadn't let her family know where she was for a good week after she had gone. Even then Rose hadn't given any details about where she was or who she was with.

"Yah, he was on leave in NeOrlins and we…well, we bumped into each other," Rose explained, pronouncing New Orleans as any native Louisianian would have done, though she left out the small detail that the meeting took place in a bordello.

"How is he getting on?" her mother asked in her soft Irish brogue. "That boy's writin' hand seems ta be broken." Lilly's brow tightened with the comment.

"He's just fine, Mom," Rose reassured her. "He looks good, and he really seems to like being in the Air Corps." But Rose's encouraging words didn't soften the frown on her mother's face, so Rose changed the subject. "So how are you feeling?" Rose asked again, setting her hand gently on top of her mother's.

"I'm doin' just fine, dear. It was all a big fuss, don't ya know. I'd a been fine right here at home," she scolded, "'stead of cartin' me off to the hospital and runnin' up such a big bill."

Gerty turned around from the sink and shook her head behind her mother's back. Rose's eyes widened momentarily when she caught sight of her sister's pantomime. She quickly redirected her attention back to her mother.

"Well, I'm glad you're home now and feeling better." Rose said with an affected smile.

"Havin' my children home is the only sort of medicine I need," Lilly said looking straight at Rose. She placed her other hand on top of her daughter's.

"Enough about me, dear. How are *you* doing? There were a few times there you really had us worried, ya know."

Rose smiled at her mother and took a long, deep breath. She wasn't sure how she would sum up two years of life-changing experiences in just a morning's worth of words. She didn't know how to explain the slow, inconspicuous, and sometimes arduous process of going from a girl—in this case a tomboy—to a young woman. And Rose was just beginning to understand the complexities of love, loss, and the true meaning of friendship. She didn't know where to start.

To Rose's relief, she was temporarily deferred from the task when young bodies and excited voices started to flood into the warm, quiet kitchen.

"Mom!" a young voice called out with a whine as a brown-haired, freckled-faced boy stepped half dressed into the kitchen. "Sean took the last clean pair of underw—"

But the boy was unable to complete his sentence when he discovered there were strangers in the room. He hastily disappeared back into the living room, but his curiosity got the better of him. He stuck just his head around the doorjamb to see who these people were. The white girl looked familiar to him, but he had never seen the colored girl before.

"Hi, David," Rose said to her brother with a soft smile.

David's mouth dropped open when he finally recognized his sister, and without thinking, he stepped back into the doorway.

Rose was wearing a white rayon blouse and simple, semi-fitted skirt, similar to what the boy might have seen his mother wear to church on Sunday. Her wavy, auburn hair was shoulder length and was sitting neatly on her head, very unlike the sister he remembered who didn't wear anything but overalls and a cap. But once she smiled at him, he knew for sure it was Rose.

"David!" Gerty yelled in admonishment. "Go put some pants on!"

David reddened and ran back upstairs, yelling, "Hey, guess who's home!"

Word spread like wildfire on that sleepy June Monday, and it didn't take long for more of Rose's siblings to rush into the room.

Next into the kitchen were Margaret and Katherine, fifteen and thirteen, respectively. Margaret, who had the same wavy hair as Rose but in a light brown shade, was tucking her white cotton shirt into her sackcloth skirt, well-worn saddle shoes still untied. Her freckled face sister, Katie, was holding a small child that Rose knew must be her youngest sibling, Rachel, who had been born seven months after Rose had left home. The two girls beamed when they saw their long-lost sister, though their enthusiasm dampened when they noticed the stranger who sat next to her.

"Hey, Rose!" Margaret finally said, running over to give Rose a hug. "You look really good!"

"Thanks! You look good too!"

Rose stood as Katie stepped up next to her, Rachel still in her arms.

"Hey, Rose," Katie said, a bit subdued.

Katie stealthily eyed Rose's friend as her sister enveloped them both in her arms.

"It's so good to see you all again," Rose said as she held them tight.

The small girl in Katie's arms recoiled at the stranger who wanted to be so close.

"I'm sorry, Rachel."

Rose stepped away from the pair to give the young child a little room.

"I am just so happy to finally meet you," Rose said with a twinkle in her eye. The little girl responded with a coy smile. Rose turned toward her mother. "She looks *so much* like Michael!"

Lilly smiled and nodded in agreement.

Rose was stunned to see how much Rachel resembled her oldest brother, Michael—the dark, wavy hair, the quiet disposition, the well that ran deep behind her dark brown eyes; it was all there.

Then Rose caught John, child number eight, peeking around the doorway. He was only four when Rose had left, so his memory of his sister was a bit vague.

Gerty walked over to John and coaxed him into the room with a gentle nudge. "It's okay, John. It's just Rose and her friend, Lilly Mae."

Sean and David skidded into the room right behind John.

"See, I told ya so," David said to his twin brother. They were identical twins and had turned nine that spring.

"Hi, Sean!" Rose said walking over to the boys and giving them each a hug. "You've both gotten so big!" she said placing a hand on each of their close-shaven heads.

The boys stood a little taller, beaming with satisfaction.

"So ya seen enough stuff? Are you gonna stay home now?" David blurted out.

Rose's body stiffened, and she felt a sudden warmth envelop her.

"David Patrick! That's not polite talk," Rose's mother scolded. "Your sister just got home." She gave her son a stern look and the whole room fell silent.

As Rose's siblings stood around waiting for someone to

speak, they couldn't keep their eyes away from the unfamiliar colored girl. Trying not to be impolite and stare, each one of them in turn made quick side glances in her direction. John was the only one who couldn't keep his eyes off the pretty, brown girl with the perfect, milk chocolate complexion.

Lilly Mae smiled at the small boy. He sheepishly smiled back then stepped a little closer to his brothers. Most of the boys had never seen a colored person up close, and they were torn between staying clear away and wanting to touch her to see if any of her color would rub off. She was a girl, after all.

Rose took a deep breath, enveloping herself in the familiar feeling of family. Now she remembered why she had come. It was like putting on a comfortable pair of overalls—soft and inviting, roomy and unassuming. A person could let oneself go here, dropping all pretense and facades, being accepted for who you were, or who you were changing into, as the case may be.

"I'd like you all to meet Lilly Mae," Rose said, stepping up next to her friend. "She's the one I told you all about in my letters. We worked together on the steamboat *Capital* and the *J. S. Deluxe.*"

Rose was pleased to have her close friend along and proud to show her a little bit more about herself through her family and her childhood home in the beautiful, rocky hills of Crawford County.

Then, one by one, Rose introduced her younger siblings to Lilly Mae, though introductions were hardly needed. Lilly Mae pretty much knew each family member by name. She and Rose had spent hours talking to each other about their families during their travels along the Mississippi. All she needed was to put names to faces. Each child gave her a polite though timid hello, the boys hardly being heard over a whisper. Then Gerty and Margaret shooed the boys out of the room so the girls could get down to more important matters—finding out what Rose had *really* been up to.

"So where's Dad?" Rose asked, as baby Rachel sat in Katie's lap and played with the waves in Rose's hair, checking out the pleasant stranger.

"He's out turkey hunting," Gerty said from in front of the sink.

"So what's New Orleans like?" Margaret asked, leaning forward in her seat, eyes wide with anticipation. Katie leaned in closer too so as not to miss a word. "When you wrote and told us you were going to school there, I looked it up in the encyclopedia at school. It sounds like a really neat place!"

"Yah, Miss Turner was happy to hear that you were going to high school," Katie added.

"And your mother was happy to hear it was a Catholic school," Lilly said with a wry smile. "Now, tell me about this young man."

A soft blush appeared on Rose's face, and without thinking she reached up to fondle the filigreed heart necklace that hung on her milky white neck. She hadn't taken it off since Malcolm had given it to her last Christmas. The fact that it was his grandmother's made it that much more special to Rose.

Katie and Margaret leaned in even closer. Gerty even stopped washing the dishes to listen in.

"He's twenty years old. He's very polite and kind and always a gentleman. Isn't he, Lilly Mae?"

Lilly Mae nodded her head in agreement, a slight smirk on her face.

"He works for himself selling people things they might have trouble finding like antique furniture or old documents. He also shops for people who can't or don't have time to shop for themselves."

"How nice," her mother said.

I wonder if she would think it was nice if she knew who he shopped for? Rose thought in amusement—namely the women at the cathouse where she lived and worked. He did this because the department stores in New Orleans raised the prices on the things these ladies needed—hose, nightgowns, even simple handkerchiefs—because of what they did for a living, so Malcolm was their buyer, and his markup was considerably less.

"Does he live with his family?"

"He has a small apartment in town, but he watches out for his grandmother who lives in a bayou just west of the city," Rose explained. "He was raised mostly by his grandmother. His mom died when he was born, and his father wasn't around much."

"And Lilly Mae," Rose's mother turned toward the quiet girl. "Rose told us in her letters that you have a big family, too."

Lilly Mae hesitated a moment, not sure what to say to the room full of strangers. "Yes'um. I got eight brothers and sisters like Rose, but I'm the oldest."

"And Lilly Mae is taking evening classes when she's not working on the riverboat," Rose explained, wanting to highlight Lilly Mae's ambitions.

"Your mother must be proud of ya," Lilly said. "Going ta school after working all day."

Lilly Mae nodded in agreement even though that's not exactly how her mother saw things. Her mother thought Lilly Mae should stay home in the evenings and help her with the children, especially after her husband had left her for good right after she had become pregnant with their ninth child. But Lilly Mae was not the loquacious type, and her tendency to clam up was exaggerated around people she didn't know, so she didn't explain further.

"And you're working too, huh, Rose? You never really did say what you do down there," Margaret said.

Rose's cheeks colored again. She hesitated, trying to think of the right words to describe where she worked. She knew she couldn't tell her younger sisters she worked in a brothel, even though it was just cleaning, some cooking, keeping the madam's books, and on rare occasions, helping schedule the patrons. Rose wasn't even sure her very Irish, Catholic mother would understand. Rose decided she'd give them a simpler explanation.

"Well…I clean and keep the books for a lady who has her own business," she finally said. "As I mentioned in my letters, she was the one who took me in when Lilly Mae and I got separated on the docks."

"That was awfully fortunate," her mother said with a serious tone. "The good Lord was watching after you, young lady."

Rose smiled. "Yes, I think he was."

"And I was sorry to hear about your elderly friend, what was her name?"

"Grandma B."

"That's right! I was sorry to hear that she had died," her mother said. "It sounds like she took good care a ya too."

"Yah, she was pretty special. Wasn't she, Lilly Mae?"

Yeah, in a sandpaper sort a way, Lilly Mae thought to herself, but she just nodded her head in agreement. Lilly Mae hadn't gotten as close to Grandma B as Rose had since she hadn't stayed in the Ville in St. Louis with Grandma's family as Rose had done. She didn't get to see her apparent softer side.

Just then the kitchen door swung open.

"Look who the cat dragged in!" came a deep, booming voice.

Rose jumped out of her chair and ran over to her father, Karl, who stood in a green-and-black checked, wool shirt, dark brown pants, and stocking feet—he had learned long ago to leave his dirty boots out on the porch. Rose wrapped her arms around his neck and squeezed with all her might. The scent of the cool outdoors and the roughness of his unshaven face were exactly how she remembered him. The tall, thin man didn't say a thing. He just stood there with his arms wrapped around his favorite girl, though he too noticed that Rose had changed. She wasn't his little girl anymore.

When Rose let go of her embrace, she took his hand and led him over to Lilly Mae.

"Pop, this is my good friend, Lilly Mae."

Lilly Mae stood and shook his hand. "Nice ta meet ya, sir," she said, barely meeting his gaze.

"Nice to finally meet you," he said with obvious sincerity. "Seems you were an awful good friend to our Rose, and we appreciate that."

The two girls looked at each other and smiled. Then Karl turned his attention back to Rose. A broad grin seeped across his face.

"I think our Rose grew up on us, mother."

"Yes, I think she has." Lilly smiled knowingly at Rose.

"There's still some batter left, Dad, if you want some pancakes," Gerty chimed in.

"I'll get it for you, dear," Lilly said, and with some effort she started to stand.

This made Rose realize that her mother hadn't gotten up since they had stepped into the kitchen over an hour ago. That was very unlike her.

"No, I'll get it," Rose interrupted. "Lilly Mae and I haven't eaten either, so I'll make some for all of us."

Both parents were amazed at their daughter's willingness and aptitude as she moved about the kitchen; this was something that she hadn't left home with. In fact, her mother had given up trying to teach Rose even the most rudimentary cooking skills. Lilly had decided Rose would eventually learn with the trial-by-fire method when she had a family of her own to take care of. And she would be there to help put out the flames.

Rose opened the kitchen cupboard to put on an apron, went to the woodstove, and threw in a few extra pieces of wood to heat the cast iron pans that sat on top of it, then moved about the kitchen as if she owned it. It took only a few wrong guesses at where the kitchen supplies were, and soon steaming hot pancakes and pork sausage sat in front of her father and Lilly Mae.

The newcomers enjoyed a long, leisurely breakfast, with the boys filtering back in now and again to catch some of the stories of Rose's work on the riverboats, of her time in St. Louis, and her present life in New Orleans. Rose managed to leave out the details of the assault her first night on the riverboat, almost bleeding to death in front of the black nightclub in St. Louis, and the police raid on Madam E.'s bordello in New Orleans. But amongst all the other colorful stories and gay experiences, there was a question that still hung in the air like a giant, white elephant but was never answered: Are you home to stay?

"Enough of all this here chatterin'. You girls must be wantin' ta get outta those travelin' clothes and into somethin' a little more comfortable," Rose's mother suggested, standing with the help of her hand in Karl's. "David, take the girls' cases up to Rose and Gerty's room, please," she said, pointing up the stairs.

"Yah, I'd like to show Lilly Mae around the farm!" Rose said with enthusiasm. "But we need to help clean up first," she continued, as she started to clear the table.

"We can handle it, Rose," Gerty assured her. "We'll get you working soon enough."

Rose smiled and squeezed Gerty's hand, and for a moment, Rose forgot her suppressed desire to leave. It did feel good to be home again.

~ ~ ~

Stepping back into the bedroom Rose had shared with her older sister felt like stepping back in time for Rose—the oak dresser with the tarnished, oval mirror that was her grandmother's and the white, metal double bed that she shared with her sister were still in their usual places. The oil lamp and worn, upholstered chair sat by the window like a sentinel waiting for Rose to pick up a book and settle in. This had been Rose's refuge, where she would sit and read well into the night about all the places she wanted to see and all the people she wanted to meet. It was all so familiar, yet it seemed so far away.

A soft breeze played with the white eyelet curtains that hung on both sides of the double-framed windows and freshened the room with the cool morning air.

The girls dressed in haste, both looking forward to getting out and seeing the countryside. Rose suggested slacks, since it wouldn't be as warm as it had been in New Orleans, and Rose wanted to show Lilly Mae all her old haunts; dresses just wouldn't do.

Rose started the tour with the farmyard. Max, the family dog, was waiting on the porch as always, along with John, David, and Sean. They wanted to tag along in order to watch the interesting colored girl and to add their two cents to the homestead tour.

First came the barn filled with scrawny cats and small, fuzzy kittens peeking out from almost every nook and cranny. Gracie and Tucker, their quarter horses, were in their stalls eating their morning ration of hay. The musty, sweet smell of horsehide and horse apples mixed with the straw gave Rose a feeling of familiarity on top of an odd hint of aloofness. This place was something she knew well, and she walked into it as if she were meeting an old friend but with a touch of disinterest that had never been there before. It was so subtle she didn't give it much import. Rose noticed that the barn was as neat and clean as ever. "A place for everything and everything in its place," her father would say. That hadn't changed either.

Just behind the barn there was the pig shed.

"We just got new pigs a few weeks ago," Sean said.

"But they're not very big yet," David added, and he picked up one of the pink and scraggly-haired creatures and offered it to Lilly Mae.

"Oh!" Lilly Mae said, cowering at the offer.

And when the piglet squealed to high heaven as she reluctantly grabbed hold of it, she knew that was a sign to let it go on its way.

Next came the corncrib and the chicken house, the latter of which had such an acrid, biting odor that it kept Lilly Mae from even coming close, despite Rose's entreaties to "Come and see the girls!"

When the tour of the farmyard was done, Rose disappointed the boys when she informed them that she and Lilly Mae were going to walk the perimeter of the farm without them. Rose wanted a little quiet time to collect her thoughts from the now-unaccustomed business of the morning.

The girls spoke very little as they walked the fencerow looking at the acres of willowy, new growth winter wheat sitting in neat, bright green rows on their right and the fatter and darker, wavy leaves of corn on their left.

Lilly Mae took in a deep breath, her face reaching up for the sun, and her countenance softened.

"This is pretty, Rose. Everything's so green! How come you never done told me you lived in such a nice place?"

Lilly Mae was enjoying the quiet landscape of the lush, green countryside, all of which seemed to be at one angle or another, very unlike the flat Mississippi delta where she had grown up. The rocky hills of this unglaciated area in southwest Wisconsin was covered in hardwoods: oaks, hickories, and elms to name a few. The farm fields were surrounded by these same trees or crude, stone walls placed there not to keep animals out but to clear the fields of rocks that were pushed up through the soil each winter. And this place had the same deep-seated calm and quiet majesty as the Mississippi river, traits that Lilly Mae was always drawn to.

Rose looked around her, and a small smile spread across her face. She hadn't really ever looked at these familiar hills like that before. She just took it all for granted.

"Smells nice out here, too. Better dan at da farm. No offense."

Rose put her arm around her friend's shoulder and grinned. "No offense taken."

Rose was enjoying the solace, as well, but it wasn't her surroundings or even being home again that was going through her mind just now; it was thoughts of her handsome Creole, Malcolm. *I wonder what he's doing now. I wonder if he misses me yet?* A soft smile appeared on her face at the thought. *Probably not,* she assured herself without hesitation. *He's probably busy finding someone that perfect lampshade for their antique French lamp, or helping Ginny with the madam's laundry. It was so thoughtful of him to take over my job so I could leave right away!* Rose was so deep in thought she hadn't even noticed that they had come to the end of the field row.

"Rose? Rose, which way do we go?" Lilly Mae asked, waking Rose out of her trance.

"Oh. Sorry, Lilly Mae. I was just thinkin' about…how good it feels to be home," Rose said.

"Yeah?" Lilly Mae said, dubious.

Lilly Mae had spent enough time with Rose to know what Rose was probably thinking about, and it wasn't about home.

"Let's go down this way. I want to show you my old schoolhouse," Rose said, pointing to their right.

This time Rose enlisted Lilly Mae in conversation in order to avoid getting caught thinking about Malcolm again. Among other things, they talked about their train trip to Wisconsin. It was a first for both of them. They had both only traveled the country by riverboat thus far in their short lives.

As the young women chatted, they walked into and back out of a small woods still damp with the morning dew. It brought them to an open, grassy area about two acres square. There a white clapboard schoolhouse stood next to two swings, two small wooden privies, and a gravel parking lot.

Rose knew the one-room school would be locked for the weekend, but she wanted to peek inside. She took a cursory glance around for something to stand on and then remembered the wooden water bucket that always sat next to the water pump on the other side of the building. Rose retrieved it, turned it upside down, and cautiously stepped on top of it to take a look inside one of the five large windows that ran along each side of the building.

When she stepped up to peer inside, she dropped right back down with a ghastly white look on her face.

"What is it, Rose? You look like ya seen a ghost."

"It's Silus," she whispered to Lilly Mae as if Silus could hear her.

Lilly Mae remembered Rose talking about her childhood friend, Silus Ripp. Rose had made it sound like they were pretty close, so Lilly Mae wasn't sure why Rose appeared so flustered at his sudden appearance. *Maybe he got maimed or somethin'*, Lilly Mae thought. She decided she'd better have a look for herself.

With some difficulty and an eventual hand from Rose, Lilly

Mae stepped up onto the overturned bucket and peeked with some hesitation over the window ledge. She saw a bushy, blond-haired young man on a ladder in front of the chalkboard with another young man with dark hair on a smaller ladder about six feet away from him. They appeared to be nailing something up above the slate board.

"They look pretty harmless ta me," she said, craning her neck a little more to see farther into the room. "Which one is he?"

"The one with the blond hair," Rose said nervously, her voice straining to keep from being heard. "But I'm not sure I'm ready to see him yet."

"Then we can just tip toe back outta hereee...."

But before Lilly Mae could finish her sentence, the bucket she was standing on tipped under her feet. She screamed out loud as her arms flailed around her in an unsuccessful attempt to right herself. Rose reached out to grab Lilly Mae but couldn't get a hold of her before she landed hard on her backside on the ground.

The two young men, hearing the scream, jumped off their ladders and ran to the window. When they didn't see anyone at first, they moved their gaze down, next to the building. They hoisted up the heavy, old windowpane, and both men peered down for a better look. They saw a young colored girl trying to stand up—Silus was sure he didn't know her—and leaning over her was a young white girl, but she was bent down helping the colored girl to her feet, so they couldn't see her face.

"Are you okay?" Silus asked.

That's when Rose looked up. If it hadn't been for her

piercing blue eyes, Silus would hardly have recognized her; she had changed so much from what he remembered.

"Rose? Rose Krantz?" he said as if he didn't know her, though he very well did.

"Silus, is that you?" Rose replied, feigning ignorance as well.

"In the flesh!"

In the flesh, indeed, Rose thought. He had grown in that flesh since Rose had last seen him; his shoulders were broader, and he had a slight, blond stubble on his chin, something he didn't have two years ago. Besides the awkward feeling she had as he hovered over her, Rose couldn't get rid of the strange, anxious feeling that had come over her when she first caught sight of him through the window. She had brushed it off as the result of seeing him unexpectedly after being away for so long.

"You look good!" she said with as much composure as she could muster.

"You look good too!" he replied with a boyish grin. "When'd you get home? I didn't even know you were coming."

"No one knew."

Then the young man, who was leaning out of the window next to Silus, cleared his throat.

"Oh sorry, Earl. This is Rose, my friend from grade school. You remember her, don't ya?"

"I would remember Rose anywhere," he said with a broad smile. "And who is this?" he asked politely, looking in Lilly Mae's direction.

"This is my good friend, Lilly Mae. She's from NeOrlins," Rose said and put her arm around Lilly Mae.

"Pleasure to meet you, miss," Earl said with a nod.

"We'll put our stuff down and come out," Silus said. He was still holding his hammer.

"Okay," Rose replied, tentatively. After the young men had ducked back inside, Rose looked at Lilly Mae with a questioning look on her face and shrugged her shoulders, eyebrows raised, eyes wide.

The young men were outside of the schoolhouse and standing in front of them before Rose could figure out what to say. Silus had grown four or five inches taller than Rose since she had last seen him, though he still was as thin as a rail. He didn't seem to know what to do with his hands, so he stuffed them in the pockets of his overalls.

Earl was stockier than Silus and just a shade taller than Rose. He wore a pair of denim work pants and a white tee shirt that clung to him, revealing well-developed chest muscles and a trim figure. He stood confidently next to Silus. He looked as if he had a million questions he wanted to ask if given the chance.

"So how long you been home?" Silus asked.

"We just got in by train this morning."

"I heard you were living in New Orleans!" he said with excitement. "I knew you'd end up in some interesting place like that."

"We were going there to visit Lilly Mae's family, and we got separated, so...Well, it's a long story. I don't wanna to bore you," she said half in jest, figuring he would press her for the details anyway.

But he didn't.

Rose looked at him with a mild frown on her face. *That's odd. I would have thought he'd want to know all about what happened. Two years ago he wouldn't have let me rest 'til he got the whole story.* And when Silus didn't ask her any more questions, she thought she better say something. She turned her attention to Earl.

"Are you from around here, Earl? I don't remember seeing you before," Rose asked.

"I'm Silus's cousin from LaCrosse. I met you six years or so ago. Don't you remember?"

Rose tilted her head to one side as she thought to herself a moment. "You're not that small, skinny kid that came to stay a couple summers?"

"Yup, that's me!" Earl said, puffing out his chest with pride.

"I wouldn't have recognized you."

"I would have known you a mile away," he said in a softer, more serious tone.

Color rushed to Rose's cheeks. She looked down at the ground, hoping it would fade before she had to look up again. Lilly Mae pursed her lips and raised her eyebrows at the statement. Then when no one continued the conversation, Rose looked back at Silus.

"So, what have you been up to?" she asked as she jammed her hands in the pockets of her slacks.

"I went to school for awhile, but I had to agree with my dad, it seemed like a waste a time since I was gonna just work on the farm anyway."

Rose looked at Silus a bit puzzled. "I thought you wanted to get away from home? You always said you wanted to go to Madison or Milwaukee and go to a trade school."

"Yeah, well, after you left, I kinda lost interest in that idea and thought I might as well just stick with what I know."

Silus dropped his gaze, knowing Rose would probably be disappointed in his choice. Rose stared at him, puzzled.

"I tried to tell him going to school was worth his time, but he just tells me I sound like his mom," Earl added.

"You know, you were always the adventurous one," Silus said. "I just kinda went along 'cause I thought it sounded like fun."

"It is fun, Silus!" Rose said with excitement. "I've seen more things and done more things than I ever imagined when I stepped on that riverboat two years ago. And I've made some very nice friends along the way."

Rose smiled at Lilly Mae and took hold of her arm. Silus looked at Lilly Mae with a questioning stare.

"Well, we better be getting back to fixin' that chalkboard," he said, changing the subject. "Mom's expecting us back for dinner, and you know how upset she gets when I'm late for a meal!" He stepped away from the women then paused. "You'll have to come by some time and say hey to the folks! You gonna be around for awhile?"

Rose looked at Lilly Mae, then back at Silus and Earl.

"We haven't really decided."

"Well, you should stop by," he said, repeating his offer as he headed for the schoolhouse steps. "Mom would love to see ya."

"Very nice to meet you both," Earl said with a nod, lingering momentarily in Rose's direction, less eager to retreat then Silus seemed to be.

"Nice to meet you again too, Earl," Rose replied, demurely. "See ya later, Silus!" Rose called out as the young men disappeared behind the battered, brown doors.

The two girls stood still for a moment. Rose was staring at the front of the schoolhouse. Lilly Mae was staring at Rose.

"*He* seems different than ya said," Lilly Mae commented.

"Yah, he seems different to me too."

"That Earl character is mighty interested in you, though," Lilly Mae teased.

"Oh, he is not!" Rose insisted, pushing at Lilly Mae's arm, trying to convince herself even more than Lilly Mae.

Rose stood staring at the schoolhouse doors a moment longer. Mostly though, she couldn't get over how different Silus was. Just two years ago he used to talk about all the things he wanted to do and the places he wanted to see. Rose wondered why he had changed his mind. *It wasn't just my lack of influence, was it?* She shook her head, trying to ignore the idea. She thought she knew him better than that.

Then there was the somewhat aloof way Silus interacted with Lilly Mae. If Earl hadn't been so cordial, Rose probably wouldn't have even noticed. She just chalked it up to a boy's awkwardness around an unknown female. Rose turned and faced Lilly Mae.

"We better be getting back home too. We'll need to help get dinner going," Rose said.

She took Lilly Mae's arm once more, and they started back for the farm.

Rose didn't say much on the way back. She couldn't get the idea of how much Silus seemed to have changed off her mind, how much everything had changed. Being home just wasn't turning out as Rose had envisioned.

2

The Illness

Gerty stood over Rose in the dark bedroom and gently shook her sister.

"Rose! Rose! Come quick. Mom's having trouble breathing again," she said in a whisper, trying to avoid waking Lilly Mae.

It didn't work. Lilly Mae woke up at the anxious sound of Gerty's voice.

Rose's eyes popped open when she heard the urgent words. She threw off the covers and dropped her bare feet to the worn, braided rug.

"What…what's the matter?" she asked, attempting to blink the sleep out of her eyes and the fog from her brain.

"Mom can't stop coughing, and she can hardly catch her breath," Gerty answered with obvious trepidation.

Rose stood and followed Gerty out of the room. Lilly Mae threw on a housedress over her nightgown and followed right behind.

"Dad's trying to convince her she needs to go to the hospital," Gerty continued as they hurried down the dark, narrow stairway toward the soft light that emanated from their parent's room. "But she doesn't want to go!"

Rose could hear her mother coughing even at the top of the steps. When they walked into her parents' bedroom, Rose saw Lilly sitting on the edge of their bed, bent over a pot of steaming water. She held a handkerchief to her mouth, as her husband held a towel over her head to help catch the steam.

Karl turned when the three girls entered the room. Rose wasn't sure if it was the steam or if those were tears that filled her father's eyes.

Rose realized in that moment that the man she knew all her life to be strong and stoic, at even at the saddest of occasions, was collapsing under the weight of the very real possibility that he was losing the love of his life.

Rose's eyes welled with tears as she ran over to her parents' side.

"Thanks for comin' down, Rose. I remembered you worked at that doctor's clinic in St. Louis, so I thought maybe..." his voice trailed off, the words caught in his throat.

Rose looked into her father's pleading face, and without a word being uttered, she knew what he was asking of her. She wiped her eyes with the sleeve of her nightgown, took a deep breath, and knelt down in front of her mother.

Looking into Lilly's pale, strained face was like a douse of cold water for the girl. Rose froze in wide-eyed shock. One of Lilly's hands was propped on her thigh as she coughed incessantly, her eyes wet, and red from the strain. When she wasn't coughing, her chest heaved and wheezed as she struggled to take in air. Her mother's anxiety was palpable; it was written all over her face. Rose's initial paralysis turned resolute as she looked into Lilly's blue-green eyes.

Rose placed her hand on her mother's abdomen. "Mom, listen to me carefully. You need to breath into my hand," Rose said as calmly as she could despite the tightness in her own stomach. "Try and push your belly into my hand as you breathe in," she ordered, remembering the elderly patient she had seen in Doctor Greenwall's clinic one Saturday morning over a year ago.

Rose had worked almost every Saturday in the medical office of Monica's father, her good friend in St. Louis. She had started out helping with the doctor's books, but when they both discovered Rose had a skill for working with patients, he hired her on as his Saturday morning assistant. The woman that had come in that day was considerably older than her mother, and at the time she had frightened Rose. She sat in the doctor's waiting room bent over and coughing so hard that on occasion her thin, white skin would turn a pale shade of blue.

Both women's anxieties were quelled that Saturday when the good doctor coolly, and with great skill, settled the old woman's breathing with his firm, steady voice, using the same remedy Rose was trying to apply to her mother just now. It seemed to be working.

Lilly looked into Rose's steady eyes and tried to comply.

She was able to slow her breathing down a small amount, allowing her abdomen to raise and lower Rose's hand until another bout of coughing overtook her.

Gerty walked carefully into the room with a new pot of steaming water. Lilly Mae followed close behind with a hot teakettle. Gerty replaced the cooling pot in front of Lilly with the hot one, then Lilly Mae filling it further from the teakettle.

After Gerty had set the pot down, Rose turned to her to give her further instructions.

"Gerty, go get the Vicks out of the bathroom. Lilly Mae, get a saucer out of the kitchen cupboard," Rose ordered, with obvious authority. The young women complied without hesitation.

Karl started to unbutton his wife's dressing gown, assuming that Rose planned to put the Vicks on her chest as Lilly did when her children had colds. Rose put her hand on top of his. He stopped what he was doing.

"We're going to use it with the steam, Dad. It works better that way."

Gerty thought she saw a slight tremor in Rose's hand as Rose took the greasy, pale salve and smeared it on the edge of the saucer. Then she knew that Rose's outward, steady demeanor was hiding the same fear that she herself felt. She had a new appreciation for her little sister at that moment; she could tell she had truly grown into a young woman. Gerty put her hand on her sister's shoulder as Rose held the saucer over the steaming water and under her mother's nose.

As Rose looked up to see who was touching her, she noticed six small faces all squished in her parent's doorway, staring blankly into the room. Even little Rachel seemed to know something serious was going on; she sat perfectly still in

Katherine's arms. Rose gave the saucer to Gerty and stepped up to Lilly Mae, leading her toward her obviously frightened siblings.

Rose knelt down and looked into their solemn faces. "Mom's having a little trouble right now," she said, trying to steady her voice. "But Gerty's giving her some medicine that will help."

She knew this was not a time to lie to them and say that things were all right. It was obvious to all of them that it wasn't, and Rose needed them to trust her and do what she said.

"Now, I need you to help Mommy and Daddy." She took John's hands in her own and looked into their eyes one by one. "The best way you can help Mommy right now is to go into the kitchen, and be very quiet."

Rose could see tears welling in Katherine's eyes, which drew a lump in her own throat. She had to take a deep breath to collect herself in order to go on.

"Lilly Mae and Margaret are going to take you to the kitchen and get you something to drink. When Mom is feeling a little better, we'll come in and let you know."

David looked straight at his sister and with a trembling voice asked, "Rose, should we say a prayer?"

Rose smiled and touched his soft, ruddy cheek. "Yes, David. That's a very good idea. You should all say a prayer." And at that, Rose stood and blinked the moisture from her eyes as her brothers and sisters pressed in on her, tears flowing and noses sniffling.

Rose turned to Lilly Mae as her friend was wiping a tear away from her own cheek. Rose gave Lilly Mae a hug, lingering there just a moment. Then she took another deep breath and turned toward her mother. Margaret and Lilly Mae herded the frightened children into the kitchen.

Rose knelt down next to her mother again and placed her hand on her abdomen with a renewed sense of calm.

"Okay, Mom, remember, breathe into your belly."

Her mother again complied, and after a minute or two, Lilly's brow softened as she slowed down her breathing and pulled the mentholated air a little farther into her lungs. Rose's remedy was helping, for now.

Once Rose was convinced her mother could maintain this breathing pattern, she stood up next to her father.

"Gerty, can you hold the towel?" Rose asked.

Rose led her father aside as Lilly started to cough once more. Rose saw in her father a fatigue that she knew was not just from the late hour but also from an obvious sense of relief.

"Dad, we need to take Mom to the hospital."

"I know, but neither Gerty nor I can get her to go!" He looked at her with a question in his eyes. "You need to talk to her, Rose. Maybe she'll listen to you."

Rose looked back at her father with unease. She knew her mother was a very stubborn woman. Rose remembered a time one hot, summer day when Rose was seven or eight. Her mother, the girls, the babies—Sean and David—had all gone to town for groceries. On the way home, the car developed a flat. Instead of waiting for a man to come along by chance and change the tire, which would mean waiting while the four gallons of milk and the three blocks of butter went bad, Lilly decided to change the tire herself.

Rose knew convincing her mother to do something she

didn't want to do wasn't going to be easy, but she also knew she had no choice. The alternative was unacceptable.

Gerty had taken Rose's place, kneeling next to her mother, coaching her to breathe with one hand on her mother's stomach. Lilly had recovered enough that she was now holding her own towel over her head. Rose knelt down next to Gerty and looked into her mother's now more recognizable face. Rose gently set a hand on Lilly's thigh.

"Mom, it's important that we take you to the hospital now."

Lilly took two more wheezing breaths, building up strength for her reply. "I'm…I'm better now," she said with a strained smile. "Thanks…to you." She reached out and caressed her daughter's cheek.

"I know, Mom, but that's not going to last. Pneumonia is serious business." Then Rose hesitated. She knew she needed to convey the import of her mother's decision. "If you don't go, Mom, it could kill you."

The room went totally silent. All anyone could hear was the wheezing in Lilly's lungs. Gerty and Karl stared at each other. Lilly looked at her daughter's serious face.

Somewhere under those brilliant blue eyes Lilly saw a young girl who used to run around all summer without shoes on and moan as if being tortured when asked to come in for dinner. A girl who when asked why she had mud streaks all over her face, would explain the elaborate story she had created about being a great Indian chief leading her people to war against the invading white man—always for the underdog, her Rose. Right now, all Lilly could see in those pleading eyes was a strong, confident, and smart young woman. A young woman who already had experienced things she herself knew nothing about.

Lilly had grown up in a large family as Rose had, and as a young woman, she had Rose's same desire to leave it all and see the world. That was, in part, why she never insisted Karl go out and try and find Rose. Lilly wasn't surprised when she found Rose's note next to the flour jar the morning after she had run away.

Long ago, Lilly's wandering energy was easily transferred to the business and joy of raising her children. When she had met her handsome, German husband, she was wooed into marriage with very little effort. The children came soon after and kept her rooted on the farm. But Lilly didn't want to get in Rose's way. So when Lilly read that note two years ago, she had decided to let Rose go.

Looking at her daughter now, Lilly knew Rose was right. Lilly knew she wanted to be around to hold Rose's children in her arms and tell them stories of their mother's wonderful adventures.

Lilly set her hand on top of her daughter's, the line of her lips forming subtle smile. "Okay, Rose…let's get going…before I…change my mind," she replied, haltingly.

There was a collective sigh in the room, and Rose reached up to kiss her mother's cheek.

~ ~ ~

That next evening, Rose sat on the kitchen porch steps with Lilly Mae at her side. The moon was full, and the large, gold doubloon had just appeared over the horizon, as the warmth of the day melted into the cool of the night.

Karl, Gerty, and Rose had ultimately taken Lilly to Xavier

Hospital in Dubuque. But first they had gone to Beaumont Hospital in Prairie. After Doctor Welsh examined Lilly, he decided it was best that she go to the larger, better-staffed hospital in Dubuque. The Krantzs couldn't afford a private duty nurse, and there was only one regular duty nurse on staff at Beaumont at that time of the night.

Gerty and Rose hadn't left Xavier until they were assured that their mother's condition was stable and that their father was set for the evening at his brother-in-law's home just outside of the large river town. Gerty and Rose both knew they had to get back to the children and take over the daily chores.

There were many questions when the tired pair pulled themselves from their vehicle late that afternoon, with lots of whining and crying from some very sleepy and frightened children. But they were all in bed now, and Gerty was chin deep in bubbles in the metal bathtub in the laundry room.

Sitting on the porch, Rose wore a weariness around her like a wet blanket, a weariness she hadn't felt since being on the riverboat *Capital* after Grandma B had gotten very sick. Grandma B had had a heart attack, and Rose and Lilly Mae had to take over the kitchen duties until Grandma B could get back on her feet. It was a huge undertaking for a then-sixteen year old. Yet the feeling Rose was experiencing now was more than just fatigue. There was a weight that she had been carrying since early that morning: the heavy weight of the expectations of her father and her siblings to do something to help their mother or she might die. And Rose knew it was only by the grace of God that she hadn't.

Then there was the long drive to Dubuque and the wait

while the doctor examined her mother and started the oxygen treatment after her x-ray confirmed it was still pneumonia.

Rose let herself tear up only once. It was after the doctor had told them that Lilly was going to be just fine. Then it was back to business: getting her father settled with her Uncle Clete and Aunt Minnie and trying to stay awake on the long, warm, afternoon car ride while Gerty drove them home. Once they were back at the farm, Rose felt she had to stay upbeat so as not to worry the children. And finally, there was the busywork of feeding the large family and getting them off to bed.

Both Grandma O'Leary and Grandma Krantz had helped care for the children in their absence, and Lilly Mae had agreed to stay and help, as well, even though she knew the grandmothers weren't as comfortable around a colored girl as the rest of the family seemed to be. But Lilly Mae stepped right up to the task, as Rose knew she would. Rose found out that she had even entertained the children with a few of their riverboat adventures, embellishing them a smidge as all good storytellers do—Lilly Mae was following her grandmother's storytelling tradition.

But here, sitting next to her friend, it all came rushing in: the stress of feeding and caring for her siblings; the fatigue of being up and racing since early that morning; and the small, lingering fear in the back of her mind that her mother truly wasn't better, and she still could die.

And to make matters worse, Rose couldn't help feel a twinge of anger. Not at her mother, really, just the situation that now would change her plans to return to New Orleans and to Malcolm. The guilt of it was too much in Rose's stretched state. She covered her face in her hands and began to weep.

Without hesitation, Lilly Mae put her arm around her friend

and handed her a handkerchief. Rose took the loving gesture and leaned into Lilly Mae without embarrassment. When Rose's crying was reduced to sniffles, Lilly Mae silently led Rose up to their room.

Rose dropped down on the edge of the bed as if in a stupor, her face blank and drooping. Lilly Mae handed Rose her nightgown, untied Rose's shoes, and slipped them off her feet. With great care, she brushed Rose's soft, auburn hair, humming the tune "God Bless the Child" so only the two could hear. Once that task was complete, Lilly Mae pulled back the covers, letting Rose slip in between the cool sheets. She tucked Rose into bed, moved a few strands of hair out of Rose's face, and blew out the light.

~ ~ ~

After breakfast the next morning, Rose wrote to Malcolm to let him know she wouldn't be coming home for awhile. She had talked it over with Lilly Mae, who had decided she was going to stay, too. Lilly Mae didn't want to leave her friend just yet. She too wasn't sure Rose's mother was over the hump, and she wanted to be around in case something happened.

But the thought of the loss of income for another week or more wore a little on Lilly Mae's mind. Lilly Mae's mother counted on at least half of her salary, and Lilly Mae hadn't worked for almost two weeks now. Lilly Mae promised herself and her mother in a letter that she would make it up to her when she got back home.

3

Serving Up More Than
Just Popcorn

Most everyone on the party line had picked up the phone when they heard it ring at 5 a.m. the morning Lilly had become ill. (Phone calls that early were never good news, so everyone wanted to know what was going on.) So most of the neighbors knew what was happening and were eager to help out. There were two pies and a cake on the counter, a roast and a pot of stew in the icebox, and folks were calling almost every day to ask Karl what they could do to help. But the children still missed their mother—each one of them. And no one seemed to be able to do things as well as Lilly.

That first week without Lilly went by faster than Rose had imagined. It took both girls a few days to get in the routine of sleeping in. Normally, in New Orleans, they were up-and-at-'em by six—Rose to get ready for school and Lilly Mae to get ready for work. But by the end of the week, they were both sleeping in until seven. It would have been even later if it hadn't been for Gerty and Margaret, both of whom wanted help with the copious amount of work that needed to be done with such a large family.

They didn't ask Lilly Mae to do any work, of course, but she pitched in nonetheless. In fact, Rose was surprised how much Lilly Mae was fitting right into the family routine. Rose was tickled when she saw Lilly Mae leaning on the wheelwell of the tractor while her father tilled the soil in the corn field before the plantings got too high, a place Rose had sat many a time. She could tell Lilly Mae was enjoying herself watching the swallows dive and dance around the tractor as it kicked up the moths and grasshoppers that were resting on the new, spring plants.

A few days later, Rose was totally flabbergasted when she saw Lilly Mae actually driving the tractor—a grin on her face from ear to ear. By the end of the week, Lilly Mae was even brave enough to go into the chicken coop with Rose and Margaret to gather eggs, though not without a handkerchief to cover her mouth and nose.

Saturday was still the day her father went to town to sell eggs or to exchange them at the A&P grocery store for dry goods, so the last of the eggs had to be gathered and cleaned before going to town. This had been Rose's job before she had left, so Margaret, being just a year younger than Rose, took on the vacated position. About midmorning, Karl and Margaret sat in the cab of the old, green pickup truck. Rose and Lilly Mae sat in the narrow, open bed amongst the packed wooden crates of eggs as they headed to Prairie du Chien. They set up shop outside the Prairie Bank on the main drag—Blackhawk Street.

Rose had planned ahead of time with her father that she would spend the day in town showing Lilly Mae the sights and taking in a movie. Rose had seen in The *Courier*—Prairie's weekly paper—that the movie *Crime School* was playing at the Metro. It starred Humphrey Bogart and the "Dead End Kids," so she thought it might be fun to see. They were also playing the last chapter of Flash Gordon's trip to Mars, and Rose knew Lilly Mae enjoyed that series. The plan was to leave the two girls in town after selling eggs and come back later to pick them up before supper.

Rose and Lilly Mae hit all the high points of town: the bakery—they actually went there even before they were left to themselves; the library—they couldn't leave that wonderful place without each checking out a book; St. Gabriel's—just because Rose wanted to show Lilly Mae the oldest parish in Wisconsin; and the Prairie Dairy for an ice cream treat. The flavor of the month was orange-flavored pineapple. Rose passed on the strange sounding concoction and stuck with plain, old chocolate. Lilly Mae contemplated having seconds.

Lastly, they took a nostalgic trip to Saint Fierole Island to sit by the riverside and reminisce. St. Fierole Island was the small, mostly uninhabited piece of land between Prairie and the Mississippi River. It was where the *Capital* Steamer docked when it came to town. While the two were on the island, they also stopped by and peaked inside the Villa Louis, which was the old Dousman family mansion turned museum. Rose explained to Lilly Mae that touring the lavish, historic, 1870 brick home two years ago was what gave her the idea of taking off down the Mississippi to visit St. Louis. Rose was amazed how long ago that felt. She promised they'd come back another time to take a tour. Their last destination was the movie house, and they wanted to be on time.

~ ~ ~

After they had paid their twenty-five cents for the matinee, they stepped inside the theatre and were enveloped in the aroma of salty, buttered popcorn and sweet candy. The girls stepped up to the candy counter, preoccupied in conversation. When they finally looked up to place their order, they were stymied by an unexpected yet familiar smile.

"Hello, Rose. Hello, Lilly Mae. Can I get you ladies something?" Earl asked with earnest.

Neither girl was able to speak. Both stood with mouths agape. Lilly Mae wasn't about to say anything to this sanguine stranger, and it took a moment for Rose to respond from the surprise of seeing Earl's face in such an unexpected place.

"Earl! What are you doing here?" Rose blurted out.

"I'm spending the summer with Silus, and I don't like to sit around gathering dust, so I thought I'd get a part-time job."

"That's nice," Rose replied, sincerely.

He is an industrious young man, isn't he, she thought.

"Would you ladies like some popcorn or maybe some candy? I can tell Lilly Mae has a sweet tooth," he joked, making Lilly Mae pull her hungry gaze away from the neat rows of strawberry whips, Slow Pokes, Mary Jane's, and the other colorful assortments in the glass case in front of them.

"What'da ya want, Lilly Mae?" Rose asked her embarrassed friend.

"Um, I guess I'll have some licorice, please."

Earl slid the long, red whip out on the counter toward Lilly Mae. "And how 'bout you, Rose?"

"I'll have some popcorn, please, and we'd like a couple a Cokes."

"Comin' right up."

Lilly Mae got her money out for the candy and soda while Rose fished in her purse for her cash. She set it next to her friend's on the glass counter. Earl set down the popcorn then the two sodas.

"This is on me!" he said, pushing the money back toward them.

The two young women looked at each other with blank expressions.

"Oh, no! You can't do that!" Rose said.

Rose thought it was a gracious thing for Earl to do, but she felt they didn't really know Earl well enough to accept a gift. And besides, Rose didn't want to encourage him. He already seemed more interested in her than she felt comfortable with.

"Sure I can!" he said, exuding confidence. "I work here." But Earl could tell that this didn't appease the young lady's anxieties, so he tried another tack. "If it eases your mind any, I get a discount on all the concessions."

Rose and Lilly Mae looked at each other again, both unsure of what to do.

"It just doesn't seem right," Rose said with slight hesitation, searching for the right words to avoid offending him.

Earl didn't know what to do, either. He had been thinking about Rose nonstop since he saw her that day at the school. He hadn't lied. He would have known her anywhere. He had always thought she was rather cute when he would come and visit his cousin during various summers. But now that Rose was grown, well, she was striking, and he wanted to find a way to impress her. Earl could tell, however, that this tactic wasn't going to work.

"I tell you what. You pay me what I would normally pay for this stuff, and we'll call it good." Earl took forty-five cents from the money in front of him and shoved the rest back toward Rose and Lilly Mae.

"Well, I suppose that would be fine," Rose agreed, demurely. "Thank you."

"You are so very welcome," he replied with a wide grin, losing himself in Rose's bright blue eyes. Rose looked down into her box of white, puffy kernels of corn as heat spread across her face and into her ears. Lilly Mae just shook her head in amusement, aware that neither of them knew she even existed.

"Enjoy the show!" Earl called out to them as they stepped away from the counter.

Rose looked back at Earl and forced a smile, putting her hand up in recognition without saying a word.

"Boy, somebody's got the hots for you, Rose," Lilly Mae teased her friend.

"Shhh, not so loud!" Rose said in a hushed voice, looking around with a furtive glance. "Let's just go watch the movie, huh."

They headed for the usherette who stood by the curtained entrance to the theatre.

Rose had assured Lilly Mae before they went inside the theatre that the Metro wasn't segregated, and Lilly Mae hadn't seen a sign anywhere, so she decided it was safe. Neither girl wanted a repeat performance of what had happened in the theatre in Savanna, Illinois, when they were forced to sit in different parts of the theatre. So they were both surprised when at the last minute the young lady stepped in front of the curtain to stop their entrance.

"Um, sorry, coloreds in the balcony, please," she said timidly.

"Oh, I don't think so," Rose shot back.

The girl's face turned pink, and she blinked hard a couple times, obviously unaccustomed to confrontation. *She can't be much older than Margaret*, Rose thought.

"I have never seen a colored person in that balcony!" Rose said out loud, not afraid of anyone overhearing. Lilly Mae looked around as everyone in the lobby turned their way. Her body sunk down as if trying to disappear into the folds of her dress.

The young girl looked anxious as she peered around Rose and Lilly Mae. There was a line of people starting to back up behind them. She bent down and whispered into Rose's ear.

"I'm really sorry," she said. "You know, I've…I've never had a colored come in here before, but isn't that why they call the balcony nigger heaven?"

"What's going on here?" came a booming, male voice from behind them. They all turned to see who was talking. It was Earl.

The young usherette sighed in relief, glad to see someone who could take over this awkward situation. She whispered in Earl's ear, relating the predicament at hand. His eyebrows lifted as she spoke. Earl looked at the two troubled young women standing in front of him and the row of impatient people behind them.

"I'll take care of this, Doreen," he assured her. Then he took her flashlight from her, opened the red velvet curtain, and outstretched his arm to invite the two flabbergasted young women inside. Rose took Lilly Mae's arm, since she knew she wouldn't go in any other way, and the two headed for the open curtain. The people waiting behind them whispered to each as the threesome disappeared behind the curtain.

They waited for Earl on the other side as he stepped past them with the flash light, beaming a path to light their way.

"Where do you ladies prefer sit?" he asked in his usual polite manner.

"Ah...the...middle, please," Rose stammered, and he led them with quiet resolve down the aisle to the center of the theatre.

Rose stared at this handsome young man's silhouette as he stood in front of the newsreel playing on the now lit screen. Earl had stopped and was pointing out a row of empty seats in the middle of the center row. Rose couldn't help herself from being impressed; he didn't even hesitate when he found out what was going on. But now Rose was wondering if she might have offended him by refusing to allow him to pay for their treats. She hoped he didn't think too little of her after what he had just done for them.

Lilly Mae stepped into the row without hesitating. Rose stopped in the aisle and placed her hand lightly on Earl's forearm. He became petrified at the unexpected touch as a mild vibration filled his body.

"Thank you, Earl," came the velvet, sweet voice. Then she gave his arm a light squeeze and, without looking back, stepped in behind Lilly Mae and sat down.

Earl stood stone still, gazing at Rose's illuminated face a full minute before he was able to break the spell of her unanticipated gesture. As he walked back up the aisle, he was glad it was dark in the theatre so no one could see him blushing.

~ ~ ~

That night both Rose and Lilly Mae lay awake. The moon was bright, and its blue-white light shown down on the wood floor and braided rug that lay next to the bed, lighting the room well enough for them both to see each other's faces and realize that the other was still awake. But still they didn't speak.

Just before going to bed, Rose had written a letter to Malcolm. It was the third in a week's time. Now she was mulling over in her mind what she had written him. She wanted to tell him what had happened at the theatre. The incident bothered her in many ways, and Rose wanted to at least share the part about Lilly Mae. She pushed off her omission of any details about Earl helping pay for their treats and the fact that he had escorted them into the theatre as inconsequential, though by that very omission Rose knew that they were not.

Lilly Mae was bothered by the incident too. Before they stepped into the theatre, Rose had assured Lilly Mae it wouldn't be an issue for them to sit on the main floor together. Lilly Mae should have suspected it was just Rose's blind-eyed optimism and not true fact. She realized she should not have let her guard down. Lilly Mae had gotten soft being on the farm where no one seemed to take heed of the color of her skin except young John, and Lilly Mae knew his stares were just innocent curiosity. *Coloreds is coloreds and whites is whites, and never the two shall meet*, she thought. She'd be more careful next time. *Maybe it was time to be gettin' home.*

Lilly Mae was the first to break the silence. "So, how long ya wanna stay?" Lilly Mae asked in her usual, no-nonsense manner of speaking her mind.

"Oh?" Rose said, a bit surprised at the question. "Um, I hadn't really thought about it." Then Rose was quiet for a moment. "What do you wanna do?"

There was another brief silence.

"Well, I don't really care much," Lilly Mae replied.

Rose understood that statement as Lilly Mae's attempt at being indecisive, in case Rose didn't want to leave just yet.

Rose was enjoying her time back home in some ways, but she was a little uncomfortable with the feeling that the farm didn't have the same allure it once had. She felt like a stranger somehow. It was like the family had changed when she was away. But after Rose had thought about it awhile, she knew that she was the one who was different. What happened today made Rose even more uneasy, and it wasn't the fact that they tried to stop Lilly Mae from sitting on the main floor of the theatre.

"Maybe we should head on back pretty soon," Rose finally admitted. "Madam E. is probably missing my help."

"And someone else is probably missin' ya, too," Lilly Mae said, playfully.

Rose reddened at her words. "He's probably so busy he hardly has time to think about me," Rose said, knowing without asking who Lilly Mae was referring to.

"Maybe," was her only reply.

After a brief silence, Rose proposed a plan. "If it's all right with you, can we wait until the end of this next week?" Rose said. "I just want to make sure my mom is doing okay before I leave. Besides, I think Dad likes your company on the tractor," Rose teased. "He told me that since I've been gone, he can't get anyone to ride along with him anymore. And now he's got a new pair of ears to give his history lessons to."

"You're tellin' me!" Lilly Mae said in an animated voice. "I asked him why nothin' 'round here was flat, and he went on and on about glaciers and ice flows dat missed dis place so long ago dat nobody was around ta even care!"

"Oh, he's just getting warmed up," Rose smiled. "Next you'll hear all about the fur traders and when the British attacked Prairie."

"The British attacked your town?" Lilly Mae said, propping herself up on her elbows. "Did anybody you know get killed?

"That was in 1814, Lilly Mae."

"Oh," she replied, a little embarrassed. "And how was I supposed ta know dat?"

"You weren't, but my dad will tell you all about it; just wait and see."

"I need ta go ta sleep, Rose. It's been a long day," Lilly Mae said, letting herself flop back down on her pillow.

Rose nodded in agreement. "I'm tired too."

Lilly Mae rolled away from Rose and started to snore within minutes. Rose lay awake awhile longer, having a harder time getting the day's events out of her mind.

~ ~ ~

The next morning was Sunday, and Sunday meant church. The family worked like clockwork, getting the young ones fed and dressed, the kitchen picked up just enough to be presentable—in case someone came over after mass—and everyone out the door just in time.

Rose, Lilly Mae, Margaret, and Katie all went in the Nash with Gerty, who had learned to drive last summer. Karl took the truck with baby Rachel and the boys. The boys sat in the back on a bale of hay so as not to get their good church clothes dirty, or just not as dirty.

Rose was not particularly looking forward to church—the curious eyes, the pressing questions. She knew her presence in the community was already known by most. News travels fast, even in the country. The feedmill or Ziel's tavern were two usual gathering places for the men. Ziel's was where all the retired farmers went for breakfast or coffee each morning because they couldn't get out of the habit of getting up early, and they needed to get out of their wives' hair. These places were gossip mills just as much as the ladies circle at St. Mary's of the Hills—Rose's church.

In particular, Rose knew there would be talk about the colored girl that she had brought with her. Rose knew folks would be polite, but there would be stares and whispers nonetheless. She contemplated suggesting she and Lilly Mae stay home, but Rose felt she needed to help her father and her sisters with the children, and she knew it would please her mother—a very devout Catholic—even though she wasn't there to join them.

There were a few people Rose did want to see, though: Marsha, her friend from grade school, Miss Turner, her grade school teacher, and a few of her other relatives she hadn't yet seen since she had been home.

Rose gazed at her friend as they stepped up to the front entrance of the small, white, country church. Lilly Mae adjusted the hat on her head for the fourth time since getting out of the car.

"Don't worry, Lilly Mae. We always sit in back," she whispered.

It was a compromise her mother had made to her father many years ago in order to get him to come to the services on a more regular basis versus just holidays or religious holy days.

Lilly Mae attempted a weak smile, not reassured much by Rose's words but thinking it might help some with the questioning eyes and the less-than-surreptitious conversations about the black girl in their midst. Lilly Mae had steeled herself even before getting out of the car. She had decided if Rose could sit among all those colored folks at Grandma B's Baptist church in St. Louis, she could sit with all these white ones.

They did sit in the back as Rose had promised, but it didn't keep them from all the prying, curious eyes. As word spread about the colored girl sitting in the back pew, heads turned, one by one, to steal a glance.

When Lilly Mae looked across the aisle from where they were sitting, she noticed that the young man from the movie theatre was looking in her direction. His face was bright with anticipation. It soon became obvious to Lilly Mae that he wasn't looking at her.

Keeping her gaze to the front of the church, Lilly Mae leaned toward Rose and whispered in her ear, "Don't look now, but there's somebody lookin' your way."

Rose waited a moment in hopes that the person staring might have time to turn away, but when she leaned cautiously forward, she saw Silus sitting on the end of the pew, and sitting next to Silus was Earl, looking straight at her. She sat back in her seat with a thud, eyes fixed in front of her, as her breath became shallow and her heart picked up speed.

Why did this young man bother her so? To Rose, it almost felt as if when he was looking at her, he was looking into her very soul.

To Rose's dismay, this went on all throughout the service. Almost every time she looked in Earl's direction, he was looking at her, and usually with a diminutive grin on his face. It became quite unnerving for Rose after awhile. She was never more appreciative when the service finally came to a close, as she sat red faced and sweating in the hard, wood pew.

Despite Rose's desire to linger and speak with Marsha and Miss Turner, she had decided she would head directly to the car. As luck would have it, when they filed out into the aisle to leave, Rose ended up right next to Earl.

"Good morning, Rose," Earl said, the grin still affixed to his face. Rose nodded and smiled in recognition. Then Earl leaned forward and politely said the same to Lilly Mae, who was standing on the other side of Rose. Silus, who was walking in front of them, turned around and acknowledged Rose with a nod and a smile.

"Hey, Rose."

"Hey, Silus."

The familiar childhood greetings rolling off their tongues.

"Did you have a good first week back?" Earl continued, trying to make small talk.

"It was very nice, thank you," was all Rose said. She wanted to discourage further conversation with the eager young man.

As they stepped outside onto the church steps, Rose thought she was out of the woods until she felt a gentle, yet firm grip on the back of her arm. She turned to find it was Earl again.

"Rose, can I talk to you a moment?" he asked with a serious look on his face. Lilly Mae caught the look too and just kept on walking. Earl stepped to the side of the exiting throng of suit jackets and spring hats, and Rose reluctantly followed.

"I wanted to apologize for what happened at the movie house yesterday." He was looking straight into Rose's eyes. "I haven't worked there very long, so I didn't know they would do something like that. I'm really sorry."

Rose wasn't sure how to respond. She looked out over the crowd of people as they filed out of the church, waving and saying "Hi" every now and then to people she recognized. Rose was still flustered by the attention Earl had given her throughout the service, so she took these cursory greetings as a way to buy time to compose herself and think of something to say. She wished Lilly Mae was standing next to her to give her moral support.

Rose took a deep breath then finally spoke, trying to settle her voice so Earl wouldn't suspect the fluttering that was going on in her insides.

"That's okay, really. How would you have known? I've lived in this town my whole life and I didn't even know!"

"Well, still. I feel bad." His expression told Rose that he wasn't just being polite. "I'd like to make it up to you, to both of you."

Now Rose was even more on edge. She felt the heat rise in her face, but she didn't hesitate in responding this time.

"Oh, no! That's not necessary!"

"But I'd like to. It just wasn't right."

"But you didn't have anything to do with it. In fact, I'm the one who should be making it up to you!" After Rose spoke those words, she realized what she was suggesting. She silently cursed herself and deftly changed the subject. "Thanks anyway, Earl, but I have to get going. My family is waiting for me."

Then without looking back, she stepped rapidly down the steps and toward her waiting family. When she was a safe distance away, she peered back in Earl's direction. He was walking away, shoulders slumped, head drooped low. Now guilt rained in on her and slowed her pace to a crawl.

Darn it! Now what do I do? she thought. *He was just trying to be nice, and I turned him down cold.* Rose turned and continued toward the car, sulking much like Earl. She was distracted from her self-incrimination when Lilly Mae stepped up next to her.

"So what'd he want?" she whispered, eager to find out what was said.

"He said he was sorry for what happened at the movies, and he wanted to make it up to me…I mean us."

"So what'd ya say?"

"I told him it wasn't his fault, of course, and that he didn't need to do anything," Rose replied. "You don't think that was too harsh, do you?"

"I don't, but the guy looked like you took away his toy truck or somethin'."

"Yah, he did look pretty hurt, didn't he," Rose admitted. Rose looked back toward the Ripp's car, but it was already gone.

"Ah, he'll get over it," Lilly Mae said absently, waving Rose's care away with her hand.

True, he probably will *get over it*, Rose thought.

But it would take a few days for both of them. Rose was glad she would be leaving soon and wouldn't be put in any more uncomfortable positions with Earl. Being home was even harder than she had imagined.

4

Not So Fast

After the second week without Lilly, patience was wearing thin in the Krantz home. Especially after Karl brought home the news that Lilly would need to stay in the hospital a couple more weeks, at least. With that new bit of information, Rose gave up on her idea of returning to New Orleans any time soon. Lilly Mae wasn't sure what she wanted to do.

Three days after they had admitted Lilly into the hospital, Karl had come home when he felt more assured that his wife was doing better. His sister-in-law promised she would visit Lilly every day, and Karl went back to the hospital each Sunday after mass, minus the children, of course—children were not allowed to visit hospital patients.

To ease some of the strain of the situation, Gerty decided that Rose needed to learn to drive. If their father was gone to Dubuque with the Nash or working in the field, someone else needed to be able to take the children to church or, in an emergency, to the doctor. And Gerty knew just the person to teach her.

~ ~ ~

"All right, this is how it works," Gerty started. "The left one's the clutch, the right's the brake, and the flat petal over here is the gas," she explained, pointing with her foot to the three different round, metal pedals on the floor of the rusted, dark-green Chevy pickup truck.

The two young women sat in the idling truck on the gravel road at the top of their driveway. Gerty had decided it was as good a stretch of road as any because it went straight in either direction for at least a mile before heading down a hill. Heading down the hill wasn't so bad, of course, it was getting back up with a stick shift that was a bit more difficult and not what she wanted to try and teach her sister her first time out. She hadn't mastered it very well herself.

"Now, the different gears are in the shape of an 'H'. See, it's right here on the top of the shifter," she said, pointing to the faded H pattern cut into the black knob. "First is at the top left, second is the bottom left, third is the top right." Gerty moved the shifter to the different locations as she explained their position. "And way over here," she said, moving the shifter far to the right and back with a bit more effort, "is reverse."

Then came the demonstration. Gerty showed Rose how

the clutch and gas worked together going from a dead stop to each subsequent gear as she slowly drove along the gravel ridge. Before they started down the hill, she turned the truck around, stopped it, and got out. Rose slid over on the bucket seat to sit behind the wheel, and Gerty got in beside her.

"Okay, remember what I told you, let the clutch out slowly."

Rose tried to put the truck in gear but was concentrating so hard on getting it in the right place on the H that she forgot to push in the clutch. Both girls cringed at the grinding sound of metal hitting metal as the gears came in contact with each other.

"The clutch! The clutch! Push in the clutch!" Gerty yelled.

Rose instantly complied. "Sorry," she said timidly.

"Okay, now you can put it in gear."

This time there was no grating sound, and Rose smiled to herself at the small accomplishment.

Rose had agreed with Gerty that it was a good idea for her to learn to drive, but she wasn't so pleased with the fact that it was her sister who was giving her instruction. She would have much preferred her father, but he was too busy with the farm, and if he took any time off, he would spend it visiting his wife. So Gerty it was.

Initially Rose thought it might work out all right, since Gerty had seemed to be treating her with a bit more respect since she had been home, especially after that night with her mother. She was happy that Gerty seemed to recognize she had changed, that she had matured. Now, however, Rose wasn't so sure this was the right thing to do.

Rose pushed on the gas pedal and let a little pressure off the clutch. The truck engine roared into action, but they didn't move.

"A little less on the gas and a little more off the clutch," Gerty instructed.

Rose complied, and the truck lurched forward and died.

"Not so fast!" Gerty reprimanded.

Rose rolled her eyes at her sister and pursed her lips. She pushed in the ignition with her foot, which sat under the dash just in front of the shifter, and the engine turned over slowly and started. The truck instantly lurched forward again, jostling the girls, then died once more.

"You've got to put it in neutral to start it up, or at least push in the clutch!" Gerty yelled at her sister.

"What's neutral?" Rose yelled back, losing her composure. "You didn't tell me about neutral!"

Gerty took a deep breath. "I did so, you just don't remember," she said tersely. She was mostly sure she had, anyway. Well, if she hadn't, Gerty wasn't going to admit it to her little sister. That just wasn't done.

"You never did!"

"I did so, now just push in the clutch, put it in neutral, the middle of the H, and let's try it again," she said quickly so Rose wouldn't have a chance to reply to her rebuttal.

Rose gripped hard onto the steering wheel. She was determined not to act like a child, even if her sister seemed to be heading in that direction. She could prove she was the more mature of the two.

Rose started the truck back up, pushed in the clutch, and put it in first gear once more—two tasks accomplished without error!

Again, she pushed on the gas pedal, more slowly this time, and let off on the clutch, determined to get it right.

The truck jerked the girls once, twice, a third time, but finally it was in gear and was smoothly moving down the gravel road. Rose pushed farther down on the gas to pick up a little speed. The truck engine roared but didn't seem to go any faster.

"You have to switch gears!" Gerty bellowed over the loud engine. "Put it in second!"

But with Gerty yelling and the engine straining, Rose forgot to push in the clutch and the gears made that awful grinding sound again.

"The clutch! You always have to push in the clutch to switch gears!"

"I know. I know!" Rose shouted back. "You don't have to yell!" And as she pushed in the clutch to move it into second, the engine roared once more.

"Let up on the gas!" Gerty said, correcting Rose again.

With much consternation Rose complied, then put the shifter in second, and with a little less jostling this time, they were coasting along once again. But what neither girl had realized was that they had run out of flat road. They had started to head down the steep hill Gerty had wanted to avoid. Both girls seemed to notice their predicament at the same time.

"Ohhh…!" was all Rose could say.

Gerty grasped the dashboard with one hand and pressed both feet hard into the floor in front of her. "Hit the brake! Hit the brake, Rose!" she screamed at her sister.

Gerty had been so intent on instructions for moving forward, she had forgotten to tell Rose how to stop.

Rose slammed her foot on to the brake. The tires locked and engine jerked to a dead stop. The truck slid along the gravel, kicking up a cloud of dust that completely enveloped the cab of the truck. The abruptness of the stop threw both girls forward. Gerty fell into the dash then onto the floor. Rose was lifted off her seat but didn't go anywhere since she had her arms braced on the large steering wheel and both feet pressed hard against the brake pedal. The girls choked and coughed on the gravel dust that came in through the open windows. They slowly turned toward at each other with shocked looks on their faces as they both swallowed hard, yellow dust and all, trying to push their stomachs back down out of their throats.

"What the hell was that!" Gerty swore at her sister from the floor of the cab.

Rose looked down at Gerty whose hair and eyelashes where covered with a light-yellow powder, mouth gaping in surprise.

"Gerty Ann Krantz, since when did you become a potty mouth?"

"Since my sister tried to kill me!" she said, pealing herself from the cramped space underneath the dash.

"Listen here, I was just doing what you told me."

"I didn't say slam on the brake, and any fool knows you have to push in the clutch when you brake!"

"Look who's calling who a fool? Maybe you should teach a person how to stop before you teach them how to go!" Rose shot back, eyes glaring.

"Well, if you had paid attention to where you were going, this wouldn't have happened."

"Me pay attention? Who's the instructor here? Shouldn't you be paying attention too?"

"I'm not driving!" was Gerty's prompt retort.

"Yah, I'd agree with that. Mostly you're just yelling."

It had finally happened. As hard as Rose had tried to avoid

it, there she was, age six, her big sister, age eight, and they were arguing about who was going to get out of bed to blow the lamp out. Gerty happened to be the last person in bed that night, and the rule was the last one in bed blows out the lamp, despite the fact that Rose had been reading by that same lamp before Gerty had even entered the room. Or was it when they were arguing about who had changed the twins' diapers last, even though Rose was sure it had been her. Perhaps it was the time they were taught the nasty job of plucking chickens.

Their father had lobbed off the chickens' heads and dressed them. Their mother had held them in boiling water to help get the feathers to soften, so next came the unpleasant job of plucking the hapless birds. Gerty was complaining to her mother that Rose wasn't doing it right, even though Rose had watched her mother very carefully when she had shown her how it was done. They were both right back there just like it was yesterday, bickering, yelling, posturing, never backing down even though there might be a small chance, a small inkling that the other person was at least partially right.

"All right. That's it," Gerty huffed then opened the truck door. "I don't need to take this abuse." Then she slammed the door shut and started stomping her way up the hill.

Rose turned, slacked jawed, and looked out the small, oval back window. Her sister wasn't stopping. She was really walking away!

Rose shouted out the window to her. "What am I suppose to do?"

"I really don't know," Gerty yelled back without stopping. "I'm just a fool, remember."

"Dang it!" Rose turned and hit her hand hard on the steering wheel. Gerty always knew how to get her in trouble. *How am I supposed to get the truck back home?* She wondered.

Rose couldn't get out of the truck because if she took her foot off the brake, Rose thought the truck would roll down the hill. But she also knew Gerty would make up some lame story to tell her father, blaming Rose, of course, and somehow forgetting to mention her part in all this.

Boy, did she hate feeling like she was six again. "Why do I let her get to me?" she said and hit the steering wheel again. Then she looked out of the front window and saw a tractor coming up the hill pulling a wooden wagon filled to overflowing with first cut hay. She sat up straight.

"Oh, good! I'll just flag this guy down, and he can help me. I'll be home even before Gerty. *Then* we'll see who's in trouble," she said smugly to herself.

Rose's feeling of good fortune was soon turned to mortification when she realized who was behind the wheel of the tractor—it was Earl!

"Jesus, Mary, and Joseph!" she said, repeating what she would hear her mother say whenever there was serious trouble at home. "Doesn't that guy ever stay home?" She dropped her head to the steering wheel thinking maybe he wouldn't notice her and would go on by.

She slowly rolled up the window without lifting her head then tried to watch stealthily through top of the steering wheel to see what he would do.

Earl noticed the dark-green truck sitting at the side of the road some ways off. As he got closer, he decided that they must be having engine trouble, since there was a lady walking up the hill behind it. As he got closer still, he could tell it was the Krantz truck sitting there, and there was a person still sitting inside with their head on the steering wheel. *Oh! Maybe they're hurt!*

The tractor puttered to a stop on the side of the road opposite to where the truck was sitting. Earl shut the tractor down, put on both brakes, and without hesitation, jumped off to make sure the driver was okay.

As he walked up to the cab, he thought he recognized the dark auburn hair despite the slight yellow haze it seemed to have. *But then a few of those Krantz girls had dark hair*, he thought.

"Oh dear, he's stopping!" Rose whispered to herself. Rose's heart instantly began to race. *What am I going to do?* she thought in consternation.

Earl knocked on the window. "Rose, is that you?"

Rose took a short breath and lifted her head slowly, then rolled down the window.

"Hello, Earl! How you doing?" she said with as nonchalant a tone as she could muster, a meek smile on her face. "Fancy meeting you out here."

"Are you all right?" he said with ardent concern.

"Oh, yah. Just fine," she lied.

Then to try and emphasize the point, she sat leisurely back in her seat and propped her elbow on the window ledge. In order to do that, however, she had to take her feet slightly off the brake, and the truck started to roll forward.

"Whoa!" Earl called out and jumped away from the moving truck.

Rose immediately slammed back down on the brake, jolting the truck to a stop.

Earl cautiously stepped back up to the cab and looked in with the same questioning expression. Rose's forehead was back resting on the steering wheel. She didn't look up when she saw Earl out of the corner of her eye. *Why does he have to be so nice? Why doesn't he just go away?*

"Are you sure you're okay, Rose?"

"No, Earl, I'm not okay," she said rather curtly, looking up in his direction. "My legs are starting to cramp because I can't take my feet off this brake. And I can't take my feet off this brake because I can't drive this truck. And I can't drive this truck because my stupid sister thinks I'm an idiot and can't learn to drive a stick."

Then there was silence. Earl swallowed hard at the verbal barrage.

"So no, Earl, I'm not okay. Okay?" Rose huffed at him then turned and stared straight out of the windshield, her face as cold as stone despite the steam coming out of her ears.

Earl looked down to the ground to hide the grin that suddenly overtook him. *Can this woman get any more attractive?*

Without saying a word he opened the cab door, excused himself, and reached over Rose's lap to pull on the emergency brake, which sat to the right of the stick shift. Rose immediately felt the strain leave her legs, and she let them drop limp in relief. Earl stood staring at her until she realized he wanted her to slide over. Earl got in behind the wheel, started the truck up with ease, pulled off the emergency brake, and drove down the road far enough away from the hay wagon to turn the truck around. He drove it back up the hill until they were on level ground again. He pulled off to the side of the road, cut the engine, and got out. Earl walked over to the passenger side of the cab and opened the door. Rose stared at him again, this time wondering why he wasn't taking her all the way home.

He did get me off the hill, she thought. She really couldn't ask him for much more than that. Rose would have to take her chances that her father wouldn't be too mad about coming to get the truck off the road. Gerty sure wouldn't do it. But in Rose's mind, this was better than being smashed to pieces at the bottom of the hill.

"I suppose you have to get your hay in?" Rose questioned. He stared at her from the open door.

"No. They really don't need it until tomorrow. I got it today because I was bored and wanted something to do," he said in a soft, gentle voice, a voice of caring, a voice of affection. "I'm going to teach you how to drive."

Rose's eyes widened with immediate foreboding. "Oh, no! I think I've had enough of driving for one day!"

"If you give up now, Rose, it's going to be twice as hard to do this again," he said very matter-of-factly. Then he stepped up on the running board and leaned into the cab to sit down, pushing Rose behind the wheel just to avoid getting sat on.

Rose sat staring out over the long rounded hood, hands on the wheel once more. She knew he was right. She knew she would work it up in her mind so much that just the thought of driving would seem like a mountain instead of the molehill it really should be. Rose looked back over at the placid, handsome face that was looking at her serenely, and she forced a grin. *But does it have to be him?* This was very awkward, not to mention embarrassing.

Without saying a word, she pushed in the clutch, then the ignition. The engine roared into action. She looked back over at Earl and waited for his instruction.

"Well, see there. You started that up just fine." Earl said, trying to be encouraging.

"Don't patronize me, Earl. This is hard enough as it is."

"Okay. Sorry," he replied, trying to repress the small smile that spread across his face. *She's cute, and she can stand her ground. I really like this woman!*

Earl's voice was smooth and precise. Somehow his instructions were easier to follow than Gerty's; they just seemed to make more sense to Rose. He explained how to use "finesse" when moving the clutch in and the gas out or vica versa. "It's kind of like a dance," he said. "You're good at dancing, I'm sure," he said, reassuringly. Though he wasn't deterred when Rose admitted she actually wasn't very light on her feet.

Then when he told her to listen, "Listen to the engine; it'll tell you when it's time to change gears," it all seemed to flow together. He even got her to go in reverse and up a small grade from a dead stop. He looked a little green after the latter experience since Rose had rolled backwards and lurched forward so many times he had lost count. But Earl never raised his voice or lost his composure during the whole experience.

He also managed to get Rose to relax a bit and even laugh after he told her the story of Silus's youngest brother. He had gotten sick in the back of the Ripp truck after he drank almost three quarts of Kool-Aid, one right after the other. He needed just three more Kool-Aid envelopes to enter the Kool-Aid contest to win the "big money"—$50 dollars—and "retire as a man of leisure" as he had proclaimed to everyone. And he knew his mother wouldn't allow him to waste it by just dumping them out, so he drank nearly three quarts of the stuff himself.

The driving instruction went so well, in fact, that Rose lost track of time. It was dusk by the time she pulled up in front of Earl's tractor.

There was an awkward silence after Rose turned off the engine and pulled on the emergency brake. Then they both spoke at once.

"I want to..."

They both laughed.

"You first," Earl said.

Rose took a moment to gather her words again, along with her gumption.

"I just wanted to thank you for helping me out, Earl. I really appreciate it." Rose's smile was soft as she gazed into the lake of his dark blue eyes.

As she lingered there, without thinking, she let herself in; she let herself feel what she had been pushing away, trying to ignore every time she met him. Rose knew it was there: an energy, a pull, an attraction just as sure as a magnet is pulled to metal or a moth to a flame. Her cheeks blushed, and she was forced to look down into her lap from the contact that never was physically made but was felt all the same.

Earl looked down too, but for only an instant. Something had changed. He felt it. He knew it. His heart leaped. His wings unfurled for flight. But Earl knew he needed to stay firmly on the ground lest he scare this reluctant dove. But this feeling, this change made it hard for him to sit next to Rose and not say what his heart yearned to sing, to not touch her soft, pink skin, or lean in close and swim in the light sent of lavender that he had caught just a hint of when he reached over her to put on the brake what seemed like days ago. Earl knew he needed to leave soon to avoid the temptation, but first he had something to say.

"It was the least I could do, Rose, to make up to you for the other day at the Metro," he said. "I still have to do something for Lilly Mae, though. I feel especially bad for her."

"Well, I can tell you from experience, Lilly Mae would rather you not. She doesn't like to be put in the limelight for any reason. But I'll let her know you were thinking of her. I know she'll appreciate that." Rose smiled a knowing smile. "Recognition from afar, that's Lilly Mae's style." Then a small furrow appeared in her brow.

"What's the matter, Rose?"

"I'm afraid Lilly Mae has to go home soon. Normally she'd be working by now to help her mother support their family." Then she continued in a softer tone. "Her dad left them after her mother got pregnant with their ninth child. She's only staying to help me out, since my Mom's still in the hospital and all."

"Yeah, I wanted to tell you I was sorry to hear about your Mom," he said with a somber tone. "But I'm glad she's doing better."

Rose looked at him with a curious look on her face. *How does he know how my mother is doing?*

"Oh, my aunt keeps us all informed," he explained, reading her facial expression. "I know more things about the people around here than I do my own family!" he joked.

Rose laughed. She knew Mrs. Ripp was a busybody. She was the first to pick up the party line whenever anyone got a call. You knew it was her too. She always had a piece of gum in her mouth, and you could hear it snapping between her teeth as she listened intently.

"I'm sorry to hear Lilly Mae can't stay. I can tell she's a close friend of yours."

"The closest!" Rose beamed. "I don't know what I would have done without her after I had left home."

There was a brief silence as Rose's mind wandered through the many hours she had spent at Lilly Mae's side on the *Capital* and *J.S. Deluxe*.

Earl was thinking of something else: how to make Rose happy. His face lightened as a thought came to him.

"Hey, I've got a great idea! How 'bout she come and work at the Metro? I know the owner could use the help. I'm always pulled away from the front counter to fix this or that or to put the next reel on, so an extra person to fill in would be great! I'm sure of it!" he beamed.

"Oh, that's a nice thought, Earl, but after that day, I don't think she wants to show her face in there again."

This deflated Earl a bit but did not deter him. Then he brightened once more.

"How about if she only works in the morning, cleaning up or in the film room in the evenings? I could always use help getting the reels on and off," he said looking at her hopefully.

"Well...I'm not sure, but I'll ask her," Rose replied, lifting Earl's spirits once more.

There was hope!

"Well, I better get going. They're gonna think I fell off the tractor and hit my head, and I'm wandering aimlessly in the road somewhere," Earl said.

Rose smiled at the joke, but immediately caught herself as Earl turned to leave. What Earl didn't feel in his excitement after Rose had let her guard down was the wall she put right back up again. Rose was disappointed with herself for revealing her interest in him, and she was determined it would not happen again.

Earl stood outside the window looking in. It appeared as if he wanted to say something more. He finally spoke up.

"I'm sure you know Monday's the fourth, and I…Well, I was wondering if you'd be interested in watching the fireworks with me?" he said, sheepishly.

Rose sank in her seat. How could she refuse the guy that just rescued her from sure disaster, the guy that had just taught her how to drive a stick shift, the guy that just offered Lilly Mae a job?

How could she not? She was already seeing someone, someone who had taken her job in New Orleans so she could rush home to check on her mother, who had given her the necklace she was wearing around her neck this very minute, and who was waiting patiently for her return. Rose really didn't have a choice, and she knew it, but it didn't make turning Earl down any easier to do.

"I'm sorry, Earl. I can't. I already have plans." And without looking at his sorrowful face, Rose pressed on the ignition and put the truck in gear. After four or five rolls backward, Rose finally rested the truck against the front of the tractor for support and was able to make her way slowly up the hill, sweat trickling down her side from the effort and the embarrassment.

~ ~ ~

Rose wasn't lying to Earl when she said she had plans for the Fourth of July; her family was going to make a day of it and go to the big doings in Eastman that Monday. Karl thought it would be a good distraction for the kids and a way to thank the girls for all the extra work they had been doing since their mother had been away. And if Karl had to admit it, he was looking forward to a little distraction himself.

After the adults had paid their twenty-five cents at the entrance to the park, they all stepped into a day of excitement and fun. And it was quite a day. To start with, there were six large hot air balloons to be sent up, something the children and many adults had never seen. It took the folks who owned the balloons a good share of the morning to lay them out and hook them up. And when they started to inflate them with the helium gas, most everyone in the park came to watch. It was a marvel for all ages as they slowly filled the huge, colorful canopies. Once they were all inflated and perched in the sky like large candy drops, the small, two-person baskets detached themselves from their earthly tethers and floated effortlessly into the bright, blue sky to the cheers of the crowd below.

But that wasn't all there was to see and do. If the boys weren't laughing at the slapstick antics of roving circus clowns, they were climbing all over the old 1920s fire engine that was on display. This was particularly true for the youngest, John. After almost thirty minutes on the fire engine, Rose had to bribe him with cotton candy to get him onto something else. David and Sean spent most of the two bits their father had given them on carnival games, especially the one that required shooting the moving, metal animals or knocking down the tower of wooden milk bottles with a ball. Being twins, they were always trying to outdo each other. Competition was just a way of life for them.

Margaret took baby Rachel on the miniature train that circled 'round and 'round on its small, oval track. There was a long line for the merry-go-round since it was free, but once they got on, everyone enjoyed the musical ride, even the twins. When it got to be four in the afternoon, Gerty met up with her long time beau, Sam Rybarczyk, and they were off to the Palace Ballroom to dance.

Katie, with Rachel in tow, Margaret, Rose, and Lilly Mae eventually made their way over to the Palace as well. They stood at the large, open double-doors looking for their sister and watching the couples float effortlessly across the worn wooden floor to the big band music of Artie Shaw or Glenn Miller. Rose became glassy eyed when they started up "Moonlight Serenade," dreaming of the night the girls at the bordello had gotten her all dolled up. Madam E. had rented a carriage and purchased tickets for her and Malcolm for the St. Charles theatre. Malcolm had a surprise of his own that night. He had taken her to a nightclub on Bourbon Street after the show, and they danced together to this same song with some Louie Armstrong and Duke Ellington mixed in.

Lilly Mae snapped her fingers in front of her friend's face to get her attention.

"You-hoo, Rose?"

Rose startled at her gesture. "Oh, sorry."

"Don't look now but you-know-who is comin' in fast," Lilly Mae whispered to her friend, pointing inconspicuously to their right. Of course, it was none other than Earl Hadwig and Silus Ripp.

"Fancy meeting you ladies here," Earl said with a charming smile. The four girls turned and smiled back. "I guess this is the place to be."

"I guess so," Rose responded somewhat reluctantly.

Margaret became doe-eyed when she caught sight of Earl's rugged facial features and trim, strong figure, and she gave him a coquettish smile. Being fifteen, she was aching for a boy, almost any boy, to ask her to dance, and she thought Earl would be a particularly nice one to start with. Katie, on the other hand, was just the opposite; she held Rachel a little tighter for fear these older boys would say something to her and she would have to say something intelligible back. At thirteen, boys were both a fascination and a fear, but mostly the latter. Katie just stood in the background and watched her big sister Rose interact with the young men. She thought it was peculiar that Rose seemed so aloof to their obvious interest.

"Did you catch us in the tug-a-war?" Silus asked Rose.

"No, I guess we must have missed that."

"Petey and Mitch were there. You remember them from school? And Earl here, he was our anchorman," Silus boasted, hitting Earl hard on the back, though it didn't seem to faze him.

The girls just smiled back. Rose didn't want to keep the conversation going, so she didn't reply. Lilly Mae was her quiet self, and she noticed that Silus didn't seem to even notice she was there. Margaret just tilted her head and sighed, and Katie and Rachel looked on in silent detachment.

As they all stood looking at the dancers, a Duke Ellington tune ended and a polka began. Earl brightened and turned toward the group of girls. "These women don't want to talk about the tug-a-war, Silus, they want to dance!"

Rose's face instantly flushed at the suggestion.

"You…wanna…dance, Rose?" Silus asked, rather awkwardly.

Silus wasn't really sure if he wanted to dance with someone he used to pal around with as a kid and who was obviously now a young woman, but he thought it was the polite thing to do. Besides, he had a question he wanted to ask her that he couldn't ask in front of everyone else.

Earl's shoulders sank. Silus had beaten him to the punch. But he knew from his conversations with Silus that his cousin didn't have any interest in Rose, so Earl would be patient and wait his turn. He knew it would be worth the wait.

Earl wasn't the only one disappointed. Margaret's shoulder drooped when Earl failed to look her way.

"Uh...sure...I suppose," Rose replied.

Rose had the same awkward feelings as Silus, but she knew if she didn't dance with him, she'd have to turn Earl down again, and she didn't have the heart to say no to him a third time.

Earl and the girls all stood in the open doorway as Silus and Rose were picked up in the sea of swinging, twirling couples circling the large room with gusto.

Rose and Silus both knew how to polka, of course. There wasn't a wedding reception or church dance that didn't play at least four or five polkas in an evening. And there were always elderly aunts or grandmothers looking for someone to dance with, since they had given up on dancing with their spouses but once or twice in an evening if they were lucky. That was never enough for these energetic women, so the young ones were typically enlisted to fill in.

There wasn't much said by the voyeurs who stood at the door of the ballroom until Margaret broke the ice.

"I'm in the running for the Crawford Dairy Queen," she boasted to Earl.

"That's nice," he said, then turned his attention back to the dance floor.

When he didn't make any further inquires, Margaret crossed her arms, pursed her lips, and started brooding. Silence overtook the group once more, until Earl remembered he wanted to ask Lilly Mae a question.

"Hey, Lilly Mae, did Rose mention that we have a job opening at the Metro? We could sure use your help!" he said, diplomatically, hoping it would be easier for her to say yes if she thought her help was really needed. And it was, sort of.

"Yeah, she did mention it," was all Lilly Mae said in reply.

"So what do you think?"

"Well...I don't think the other folks at the theatre would like a colored workin' there," she said in her usual straight manner of speaking. "I haven't exactly been greeted with open arms since I been here. In town, I mean," she said, correcting herself. "Rose's family's been nothin' but nice, a course."

There was the movie incident, of course, but it was more than that. The whole day that Rose and Lilly Mae toured Prairie du Chien, everyone they met looked at Lilly Mae as if she had antennae sticking out of her head. Then there were the little children who hid behind their mothers and pointed saying, "Mommy, look, a darkie" or "Mommy, look, a colored." Or if the children hadn't learned the normal nomenclature of the day, they described her as "that brown girl." Most of the people in Prairie had seen colored people like Scott Joplin or Joe Louis in the paper or in the movies, but many had never seen a colored up close. The only time they might catch sight of one was from a distance, working on a barge or on an excursion riverboat.

"I know Prairie's not like New Orleans, but it would just be you and me most of the time. I need help cleaning up in the mornings after the shows, and if you want to work more hours, you could help me setting up the reels for the evening and gettin' the concession stand ready before we open the doors."

Lilly Mae was silent. Earl could tell she was thinking.

"*I'd* love to work with you, Earl," Margaret chimed in when Lilly Mae didn't appear to be answering him. *Anything to spend time around you*, she thought as she smiled hopefully at him.

Earl just smiled reticently back without a reply, then turned again toward Lilly Mae.

"It would really help me out!" he pressed her. *And impress Rose at the same time*, he thought.

Lilly Mae was contemplating her answer when the polka tune ended and couples started exiting the ballroom to get some much needed air. The small group stepped back to let the rosy-cheeked couples pass.

"Well, just think it over," he said as casually as he could over the voices of the passing crowd. "You can start whenever you want. Just have Rose give me a call." Then he turned toward his friend and Rose as they came toward the small group. He noticed both of them had a look of consternation on their faces.

"Let's get going, Earl," Silus said abruptly and walked on past without stopping to say goodbye.

Earl looked bewildered at Rose but didn't think it was prudent to question her at the moment. With that look on her face, Earl could tell she obviously wasn't in any better mood than Silus.

"Oh...well...see you ladies later," he said, tipping his cap and bowing slightly. Then he took off after Silus, who was already a good ways off.

"Ahh...Rose, you scared him off!" Margaret complained to her sister.

"What are you talking about?" Rose asked unaware of her sister's pining. Rose had more distressing things on her mind.

"You scared Earl off with your sour puss," she clarified.

Rose didn't reply after she caught the sappy, mournful look on her sister's face. She just shook her head in disbelief and turned her mind to more important matters, like what her old, best friend had just said.

5

When the Blinders Fall

As the impending night darkened the landscape, blending the hard edges of color and form into muffled blacks and grays, the crowd descended on the ballpark. This was where everyone went to watch the fireworks display. There was a slow mixing of bodies and voices moving to the field, as families picked out just the right spot to lay down their blankets. As the children waited eagerly for the night's entertainment, the adults enjoyed the setting sun as it changed the horizon from orange to red, then purple and gold, and finally into multiple shades of gray, lighting the clouds overhead in an almost northern lights type display.

When it became dark enough, the children wrote their names in the air with gold and silver sparklers, while gangs of adolescent boys ran around menacing the crowd. Their usual targets were the gaggle of young girls that roamed the infield, stuck together like glue. Their ranks were parted only after the boys threw some type of firework, usually firecrackers, in their direction. The boys would then run just far enough to stay out of catching range but close enough to watch the girls' reactions; screeching and running was the most prized.

The outside edge of the field was always the unofficial lover's lane for the evening. The young boys rarely ventured there. But if they were brave enough and thought themselves fast enough, they would run along the outside rim of the field and lob a stink bomb or firecracker above the lover's heads. They hoped they could run faster than the strong, young men sitting next to their sweethearts. The boys knew the penalty if caught: a wedgie or at least a good, swift kick in the backside. Of course, Gerty was sitting there with Sam, and it had been arranged that the family wouldn't see her again until they got home.

The rest of the Krantz family and Lilly Mae were on a blanket in the middle of the field. The grass just behind the pitcher's mound was their mother's spot each year, so, of course, that patch of ground was quickly agreed upon with a slight pang of regret in everyone's heart.

It had become Karl's job to pick up fireworks for the children at the Ben Franklin store, though most years he remembered only with the aid of his wife. This July Karl was on his own.

Rose helped Rachel hold a sparkler in her hand, though this didn't last too long. Rachel didn't like the slight sting the sparks gave her as they hit her soft, delicate skin'

The tangy smell of smoke from the festivities filled the air and floated softly in the evening breeze, creating an undulating haze that danced around the ball field. Above their heads, thicker clouds had rolled in soon after dusk, which darkened the sky more than normal and brought cooler air and a tinge of dampness that seemed to promise rain.

The family huddled together on the blanket in the pitch-blackness to try and stave off the cold. Karl went back to the truck to pull the old blanket off the seat so the children would have something to cover themselves with. *Lilly would have remembered to bring extra blankets*, he said to himself in reprimand. He was missing Lilly too.

There were murmurs of rain as he walked through the crowd and questions of "would the show go on," until the first, chest-pounding thump was heard, immediately followed by a burst of color in the black sky above amid the "Ooos" and "Ahhs" from the spectators below. All weather predictions were quickly forgotten.

Applause erupted after the grand finale and just in time; a drizzle had started to fall. Everyone hastily picked up their blankets, wrapping their small ones inside them, and walked at a rapid pace toward their vehicles. When they were about halfway to the parking lot, the sky opened up, and it started to pour. There was a mad rush to get in, out of the rain. Karl took Rachel, Margaret, and Katharine with him in the truck. Rose took Lilly Mae, David, Sean, and John in their mother's Nash. Rose had gotten a crash course in driving the car just that morning from her father. It was a piece of cake for Rose compared to the truck, since it was an automatic.

"Oh my!" Rose declared once they were all finally in the

car. The boys giggled and shook their hair at each other in an attempt to make each other even wetter than they already were. Without warning a streak of lightning lit up the sky, and not a second later a deafening clap of thunder silenced the whole group.

"Wow, that was close," Sean said with awe.

"Not even a mile! I don't even think I got to one thousand-one!" David added.

"You know that don't work," Sean chided his brother.

"It does so. Dad said so."

"Well, Miss Turner said it isn't true," he corrected him again.

"Is so!"

"Is not!"

"Is SO!" David said a little louder, leaning chest first into his brother.

Being brothers, fighting and arguing was what one did. But because they were twins, they seemed to have a particular need to be different, better, more accurate...then their counterpart. That's why, since age three, they were put at opposite ends of the dinner table, one next to each parent.

Then another flash of lightning and the simultaneous clap of thunder illuminated the sky, and folks were running and slipping through the now-muddy parking lot to their cars and trucks.

"See there, God doesn't want you arguing anymore, and neither do I, so let's just try to get along until we get home," Rose pleaded, turning on the ignition.

She fumbled to find the switch that started the wiper blades to try to part the river that was streaming down the windshield. Rose wasn't all too comfortable with this situation. Driving home at night was going to be bad enough since she had never driven in the dark before, but driving home at night in a torrential rain made her more than a little anxious.

"I'm just going to wait a little while, until some of these cars leave, before we head out, okay?" she said to the boys. They let out a collective whine and slumped in their seats.

"Hey, I know! Let's sing a song!" Rose suggested cheerfully to the less then receptive crowd in the back seat. But when she started "Camp Town Racers" and got to the "do-da" part, the boys started in with enthusiasm. Then came "I've been Workin' on the Railroad," and lastly they sang "She'll be Coming 'Round the Mountain." By this time most all of the cars had left the parking lot, so Rose turned on the headlights and put the car in gear. The tires spun a bit in the mud but eventually they took hold, and Rose crawled slowly out onto the now very rutted road.

Lilly Mae kept the boys busy singing, this time it was "Short'nin Bread," to keep them from fighting, but mostly to try and keep herself calm. She was even less convinced of Rose's ability to drive in the pouring rain than Rose was.

The thunder and lightning continued, and the rain was coming down in sheets. Rose was having trouble seeing in front of her. The wipers didn't move fast enough to keep the windshield completely clear. On top of that, the road was a slick, muddy mess, so she moved along rather slowly. The boys were getting impatient.

"When are we getting home?" John whined. "I'm cold."

"I'm cold too," Sean added. Their wet clothes were starting to wick the heat away from their small frames.

"Not as cold as me!" David shot out.

"Am so!"

"Are not!"

"Okay, okay! Now listen here boys. I really need you to behave right now," Rose said as she gripped harder to the steering wheel. "I need to concentrate on the road. Okay?"

There was a group mumble in agreement, and the boys reluctantly settled down, though the peace didn't last long. Soon there was a shrill cry from the back seat with the accusation of someone having pulled someone else's hair. Furious, Rose wheel around in her seat, and when she did this, she inadvertently turned the steering wheel to the left.

"Rose, look out!" Lilly Mae shouted out.

Rose quickly turned back to face the road, realizing what she had done when she saw a pair of large, round headlights heading straight for them.

"Dear God!" she yelled out as she jerked the wheel hard in the opposite direction.

With this, everyone in the car was thrown to the left. Unfortunately, Rose had overcorrected, and with the wet, slick slurry that was now the road, they were off the road and heading down into a steep ditch, everyone in the car screaming in fear!

They stopped abruptly when they hit bottom, breaking a headlamp and bending the car's bumper. Rose had been thrown into the steering wheel, and the horn blared from her weight lying against it. She had hit her head on the frame of the windshield so hard it took her a moment to realize where the sound was coming from and what had happened. When Rose heard whimpering from the back seat, she instantly woke out of her daze and leaned over the seat to find her brothers in a heap on the floor all crying softly.

"Jesus, Mary, and Joseph, what have I done?" She looked

over at Lilly Mae who was pulling herself from underneath the dash.

"You okay, Lilly Mae?" Rose's voice an octave higher than normal.

"Had ta take us for one more carni' ride, did ya?" Lilly Mae joked.

Rose climbed up over the front seat and helped her brothers off the floor. Rose put John on her lap and pulled Sean and David in close. Rose rocked the crying group side to side.

"We're all okay," Rose said reassuringly.

She was not only trying to comfort her brothers but was trying to steady herself, as well. As she sat there holding those small, wet bodies, she realized how lucky they all were. *We could have been hit by that car, or hit something other than the bottom of a ditch*, Rose thought to herself, and she gave her brothers another squeeze.

It had been a trying couple of weeks for Rose with her mother away. It meant so many mouths to feed, clothes to clean, dishes to do, and children to care for. Rose never realized how hard her mother and sisters worked. And to top it off, Rose missed her mother just as much as the rest of the family. A small tear trickled down Rose's cheek. She bit her lip to keep herself silent in front of her obviously shaken siblings and held them tight.

As they were sitting there with the engine still running and the rain still pelting down on the roof of the car, the inside of the car was illuminated from behind. They all looked out through the foggy rear window at a pair of round headlamps above them. Before they could react, they were startled by someone knocking on the back door window.

"Is everyone all right in there?" came a masculine voice.

"Yes, yes, we're all right!" Rose called out.

She set John down off her lap and crawled over David as the passenger door opened and a man stuck his head in to see the five anxious faces.

"Oh my God, Rose! Are you all right?" the young man said in excitement when he recognized who was in the car. It was Earl.

"Oh Earl!" was all Rose could say as she reflexively grabbed hold of his forearm and held on tight. It took her only a second to realize what she was doing, and she instantly dropped away from him.

Earl looked past Rose at the young boys beside her. "How you guys doing? Helpin' your sister out, I can see," he said to bolster their spirits. "You okay, Lilly Mae?" he asked, glancing in the front seat.

Lilly Mae nodded her head in silent acknowledgement. Then he faced Rose again. "It's still pretty nasty out. I would suggest we leave the car here, and I'll help your father come get it in the morning."

Earl went around to the driver's side of the car, opened the front door, and turned off the ignition, killing the remaining headlamp. He helped Rose get the boys, Lilly Mae, then finally Rose herself up the slippery ditch to the inside of his warm truck. It was a tight squeeze, but they all made it inside. Earl laid out the blanket that he had used at the fireworks over their laps, and they headed for the Krantz farm in damp, shivering silence.

~ ~ ~

Earl sat in his stocking feet at the warm kitchen stove drinking coffee with Rose's father, steam wafting off his wet shirt and pants. Karl had started up the stove to heat some coffee for the young hero and to shoo away the dampness. Rose and Lilly Mae had taken the boys upstairs, and with the help of the other girls, dried them off and put them to bed. Rose and Lilly Mae had already changed into their nightgowns when Rose remembered Earl was still down in the kitchen.

"I'm going to go ask Earl a quick question," Rose said as she put on her sister's robe.

"'Bout what?" Lilly Mae asked.

"I'll tell ya later," Rose answered hastily, before she ran out of the room.

Rose found the two men sitting by the kitchen stove swapping hunting stories by lamplight. They both stood when she walked in.

"Well, I best be headin' off to bed," Karl said, looking at Rose then at Earl. "I got a car to get early in the mornin'," he said, looking for an excuse to leave the young couple alone.

"Oh, yes, Mr. Krantz. I can help you with that!" Earl offered, enthusiastically. "Just give me a ring, and I'll come show you where it ended up."

"That'd be awful nice of ya, Earl. With Michael in the service and my two oldest boys just nine, I could use a strong pair of arms to help me out."

"No problem, sir. I'd be glad to." He shook Karl's hand vigorously, then beamed at Rose.

Karl came over and kissed Rose's forehead, something he had taken to doing since his wife had been sick. In fact, he had become more affectionate with all his children, which meant a peck on the forehead for the girls and a bear hug for the boys. The situation with his wife had made him realize how much he appreciated his family, and this car accident had just reinforced the sentiment.

"I'm really sorry about the car, Dad," Rose said, apologizing for the third time.

"I told you before, sweet pea, no need to say you're sorry. It could'a happened to anyone." Then he took hold of her and hugged her. "It was my fault, anyway. I shouldn't have let you drive in those conditions, especially since it was your first time driving at night. I just thank the Lord you're all right!"

"I love you, Pop!"

"I love you too, sweet pea." He gave her one more squeeze, glanced back at Earl, gave him a nod then headed to bed.

"Oh, look at you. You're soaked through!" Rose said with concern.

"I'm not sugar. I won't melt," Earl quipped.

"But you'll catch your death!" Rose countered. "At least take that shirt off. I'll get you one of Dad's. You can wear it home and bring it back tomorrow," Rose said as she headed into the dark laundry room.

Rose rummaged around in near darkness before she turned to stand in the darkened doorway, looking back into the dimly lit kitchen. Earl was standing facing the stove, holding his steaming shirt above it. Rose stopped and looked at his wide shoulders and the strong arms that held the wet shirt in the air. Rose had seen Malcolm with his shirt off once or twice when they were working in his Grandmother's garden or when he was delivering fifty-pound bags of rice around New Orleans. Malcolm wasn't scrawny, but he didn't have the stocky build that Earl had. Rose imagined Earl could pick her up easily, unlike the fifty-pound bags of rice Malcolm struggled with.

Rose shook her head. *What am I thinking about? I have someone patiently waiting for me down South.* She blushed at the recognition of her desire. Rose sighed at herself in disgust, settled her outward appearance (she didn't have time to calm her insides), and walked back into the room.

"This one should fit," she said as casually as she could. "I think it was one of Michael's."

Earl set his still damp shirt on a chair and took the dry one from Rose. "Thanks a lot, Rose. That's very thoughtful of you," he said with a warm smile.

His well-formed chest with its smattering of curly, dark hair made him look even better from the front. Rose couldn't hide the blush that filled her cheeks. She only hoped that Earl couldn't see it in the muted lamplight that lit the room. She knew he couldn't feel the heat he was creating inside her.

Rose promptly picked up the coffee cups from the table and walked to the sink. She busied herself rinsing them out while Earl put on the shirt. She had to compose herself. She had a question to ask him, and she wasn't quite sure how to ask it.

"Earl?" she started without stopping what she was doing. "Why wasn't Silus with you tonight, when you picked us up, I mean?" Rose had an idea about what might have happened, but she wanted to know for sure.

Earl was silent for a moment. Rose turned around.

"Well, we were walking back to my truck after the fireworks, and I decided to press him for an answer to your sudden change in mood at the dance hall. It looked like he'd upset you in some way, and I wanted to find out what had happened," he said with some restraint. "When I found out why, I was sorry I had asked."

Rose turned toward him and folded her arms in front of her, credulous.

"When he told me that he couldn't believe you were a nig..." He cut himself short and started again. "...that you like coloreds so much, I got kind'a upset and told him off. I knew Lilly Mae was a really good friend of yours and… Well, he didn't want to ride home with me after that." Earl lowered his head.

Rose was right. She knew it was about Lilly Mae. Her impression of Earl had been correct. He didn't have any problem with colored people, at least he didn't show it with the way he acted toward Lilly Mae. But Rose was totally shocked when, while they were dancing, Silus had asked her if she was doing some sort of charity work by having "that colored girl" staying with her. He honestly didn't believe her when she told him that Lilly Mae was her best friend. The hair stood up on the back of Rose's neck as she stood thinking about it.

Then Rose's countenance changed; her arms dropped, and she stared blankly at the floor. On top of everything that had happened this evening and over these many weeks, Rose realized she had just lost a good friend. It was a feeling she could readily recall: the ache in the pit of her stomach, the feeling of being lost, unsure of what to do. She was back at Grandma B's funeral again, back amongst all those people but feeling very much alone.

"Rose? Are you okay?" she heard off in the distance. Then Earl touched her arm, and she looked up to see a pair of fervent eyes staring intently at her.

"I'm sorry about Silus, Rose," he said as if reading her

mind. Rose noticed he seemed to have a knack for that. Then he tilted his head slightly and looked at her with a puzzled expression. "Did you bump your head?" he asked as he moved her bangs away from her forehead to reveal a light-pink lump on the left side of her forehead.

Rose touched a spot just below her hairline and felt a slight sting. "Oh, yah. I hit my head on something when we went in the ditch."

"Here," he took her elbow and pulled her to a chair. "Sit down. I'll get you some ice."

"That's not necessary."

"I heard you were a nursing assistant in a doctor's office. You should know better than that."

Rose couldn't argue with him. She knew ice on a contusion soon after it occurred helped decrease the swelling, so she sat quietly as Earl picked off a hunk of ice from their icebox, wrapped it in a dishtowel, and gently set it on her forehead. Rose had to admit, it did feel good, cooling her forehead and helping freeze the painful thoughts of losing an old friend.

"Um, I can probably hold onto this myself," Rose decided when she realized who was holding the ice.

"Oh, yeah. Sure."

As they attempted to switch hands around the compress, the hunk of ice fell through their fingers and dropped to the floor. They both bent down to pick it up, their faces coming just inches from each other. Earl stared at Rose, diving deep into a pair of bright blue eyes that were barely diminished by the lamp light. Rose met his gaze then broke it off abruptly, dropping her eyes and hastily standing up to step away from him.

Earl's obvious ardor fell from his face at her apparent

repulsion, slowly replaced by a look of resignation. Without saying a word, he picked up the ice and put it in the towel that was still in Rose's hand. He took his damp shirt off the kitchen chair, put his cap on his head, and headed for the door. With his hand on the doorknob, he stopped and looked back at Rose.

"I'm glad none of you were seriously hurt, Rose," he said, sincerely. "I'll bring the shirt by after it's been washed." Then he opened the door, pushed back the screen, and stepped silently out into the night.

Rose stood staring at the kitchen door. It didn't take her long to decide what to do. She rushed through the door and stepped out to the edge of the porch, the cool, wet rain hitting her warm, bare feet. She called out to the invisible figure in the pitch-black night.

"Earl, come back! I didn't get a chance to thank you!"

Without warning, seemingly out of nowhere, Earl bounded up to her, jumping onto the porch with one easy step and swept Rose into his arms. He stood over her grinning like a mischievous schoolboy before he lowered his lips to hers. Rose didn't resist. She couldn't resist any longer. She wanted to be held, she wanted to be kissed, she wanted to be loved, and Earl was more than happy to oblige.

Earl reveled in the softness of her body next to his, in the sweetness of her lips, in the scent he had wanted to capture again and again since their driving lesson just a few days earlier. And now he held it all in his arms, and he never wanted to let it go.

Then without warning, Rose pushed him away and ran to the corner of the porch to face the falling rain.

He followed her but hesitated before he lightly put his hand on her trembling arm. She flinched at his touch, then he turned her around. Her face was wet. He could tell it was not just from the rain.

She buried her face in his chest and shook gently in his arms. Earl knew it was best not to speak just yet. He knew when she was ready, she would tell him what was wrong. *It's probably the accident*, he thought, *or maybe because her mother is still in the hospital*. He had heard his aunt say that she was going to have to stay there another week. When Rose began to talk, however, he wasn't ready for what she was going to say.

"I'm sorry, Earl. You've been so kind to me. At every turn you've only been the gentleman," she said through her tears. Earl handed her his handkerchief, and she let out a quiet guffaw at the obvious example. "You helped Lilly Mae and me at the theatre, then with the driving lesson, and now tonight you stood up for my friend again, and with the car..." Rose hesitated.

The tears started to stream down her face again. She blew her nose and tried to collect herself, taking a deep, stuttering breath.

"It's okay, Rose. Really. It wasn't a problem." He tried to step closer to her, but she put a hand to his chest to hold him away.

"No. No, you don't understand. You don't deserve the likes of me," she said looking him straight in the eye. She took a deep breath then continued. "I'm already dating someone, Earl, in New Orleans. I'm away three weeks, and I can't even be faithful to him," she admitted. Then she turned away again as her shoulders began to shake once more.

Earl stood dumbfounded. He didn't know what to say. He didn't know what to think. Now he understood why she was always moving away from him, always skirting his advances.

This explained a lot to the ardent young man. He looked at Rose, a soft, angelic, shaking form, silhouetted against the dark of night. He wanted her to forget this guy so far away. He had her now, and she obviously wanted him too. *She'd get over him eventually*, he thought. He'd make sure of that.

Earl stepped closer to the trembling figure then stopped.

He placed his hand on her shoulder and again she jumped at his touch. Rose turned to face him as he looked into her red and puffy eyes. Earl decided he needed to make a confession as well.

"I have to be honest with you, Rose," he looked at her seriously. "I'm dating some else too."

Rose tried to blink the tears away, but she couldn't wipe the look of surprise off her face.

He stepped back. "I'm the one who kept trying to get close to you, trying to find ways to spend time with you. It's my fault."

"Oh Earl!" she said, rushing into his arms.

They stood holding each other in silence, each basking in what they knew was the last of their closeness, the last of their overt desire.

Earl was the first to pull away. He took Rose's face in his hands, closed his eyes, and kissed her softly, slowly on the lips. He was memorizing the touch, the scent, the woman of his dreams. Then he stepped away from her, turned, and was swallowed up by the splatter of water on the rain-soaked ground and the black of the night. Rose heard the squeak of his truck door opening then closing again, then the engine roaring to life. The headlights came on, illuminating the drops of falling rain. The truck idled just a moment before Earl put it in gear, and the two beams directed him out of the driveway and out of Rose's life.

Earl sat in his truck shivering as he drove slowly away. But he knew he wasn't shaking just because he was wet; it was the inextricable thrill Rose gave him, a thrill that he would never forget. Earl had dated other women before and even kissed a few, but being with Rose gave him a feeling he had never had with anyone else. Since that very first meeting at the school, his body did not feel like it was his own; he was having trouble falling asleep at night, and just yesterday he had to take his belt in a notch. He hardly had an appetite. Now, having been so close to her, his control abated further. He could still feel the warmth of her skin, the suppleness of her breasts against his chest, her silky, lavender scented hair as it caressed his face when he held her tight.

Then there was the kiss: the softness of her lips, the honey that was her mouth. It all was burned into his memory and would reside there for a long time to come. But right now he was hoping his lie would help her put some distance between them. He didn't want Rose to feel that her desire for him was wrong, and he wasn't going to try to convince her to forget about that other guy either. He didn't want her that way. Earl felt strangely comfortable with this dichotomy. He knew this would be better for both of them, for now.

Generally, Earl wasn't a religious man, but he said a prayer that night, a prayer that maybe, someday, somehow, Rose would be his.

6

An Uncomfortable Fit

Rose's mother did stay in the hospital two more weeks, and when she was finally allowed to go home, she was given strict orders to rest. The whole family willingly made sure the doctor's orders were followed. Just having their mother home again was enough to lighten their load.

What this meant was a continuation of the status quo: more work for each member of the family. Initially the new job assignments were met with little resistance. John's normal job was hauling wood for the kitchen stove. With Lilly gone, he took on the added responsibility the twins normally had of keeping the pigs fed. David and Sean were given the task of weeding the garden, even though they argued that it was women's work. This was in addition to their normal job of helping their father with the farm. Margaret and Katie, with the occasional assistance of Rose and Gerty, were the laundresses and were in charge of keeping Rachel out of trouble, which they did most of the time, anyway.

Rose and Gerty were the chief cooks and housecleaners. Lilly Mae surprisingly agreed to help Margaret with the chickens, keeping them fed and the eggs collected and cleaned. She even learned all the names that Margaret had given each of them, though she couldn't force herself to sweet-talk them as Margaret normally did. She was more likely to throw in a few epithets under her breath than endearments at the unpredictable, yet winsome foul. Chicken duty was in between helping Karl in the fields (her favorite job), the twins in the garden, and the girls in the house. Being the oldest of nine, Lilly Mae was no stranger to work, so she pitched in wherever help was needed. And so the summer days passed.

$\sim \sim \sim$

The passage of time on a farm isn't measured by days or weeks as much as by the rhythm of the earth. The spring, of course, is busy with turning up the soil and planting, both the fields and the family garden, the latter of which needed to be large in order to feed the many mouths that sat around their table. The more you grew and "put up," the less you had to buy. This was not so much a product of the Depression as it was the way things were done on a farm. This way of life actually seemed to ease the hardship on farm families that the Depression had brought more acutely to their urban counterparts.

Mid to late June was berry season. It started with large glass bowls filled with succulent, red strawberries sitting on the kitchen counter. Lilly didn't grow strawberries herself, but she always insisted they get just enough from the neighbor's patch to make a few jars of jam, since it was her husband's favorite. The neighbor wouldn't let her pay for them, of course, so it was agreed that Lilly would supply them with the red raspberries that they didn't grow but Lilly did.

Soon after the strawberries were gone, the black caps were ripe, so the children donned their long sleeves and slacks, despite the warming sun, to pick the deep-purple berries amongst the sharp, thorny stems. They were hidden all over the farm. It was always a game of who could find the biggest patch. Their larger, domestic cousin, the red raspberries, grew in neat rows at the far edge of the garden, and what wasn't put up as jam or jelly or given in exchange to the neighbors was sold along with the eggs in town.

The rhubarb would grow from late May into August if watered regularly, and it kept the family in rhubarb sauce, rhubarb pies, and rhubarb cakes for many months. It was almost as prolific as the zucchini squash and cucumbers.

Lilly enjoyed the tang of elderberry jam, so when the small white bunches of blooms came out in June, she made sure the children took note of where the normally nondescript plants were growing. She also knew her husband would most likely make another batch of elderberry wine—his mother's favorite.

September brought grapes, which were in abundant supply at the Krantz home. Karl had built the arbor for his wife behind the house, along the edge of the pasture, the year they were married. Along with making more jelly out of the deep purple fruit, the family also canned a couple dozen quarts of the juice. It would be a savory, tangy treat in five or six months when the snow was flying and all that was green and sweet was mummified by the cold.

The sweet corn was plump and ready for picking in August. It needed to be picked by hand, so it was an all-family job. What wasn't eaten was canned. What wasn't canned was sold in town. Canning corn was almost as messy a job as making jelly, but with the boys shucking and the girls boiling, cutting, and canning the corn into glass mason jars, they were done with all the family would need in a couple of days.

Occasionally Rose felt like these tasks were beginning to feel like a burden for all involved. So periodically she tried to lighten the load with the occasional trip to the dairy or to a movie show in town. *Snow White and the Seven Dwarfs* had come out that July, and the amazing color and charming story even kept small Rachel mesmerized. Later Rose would take Lilly Mae and the boys to *The Adventures of Tom Sawyer*. She had to restrain Lilly Mae from making corrective comments about river life throughout most of the film. Most of the time, however, Rose enjoyed the camaraderie of the shared tasks and the fun that usually went along with them—that was, until it was time to harvest the wheat.

~ ~ ~

It was midsummer when the winter wheat turned to a sea of deep, burnt gold. Lilly had been home for only a couple of weeks, and for the women of the farms, this meant the large task of feeding the cutting and threshing crew that went from farm to farm to bring in the different grains. She would need all her girls to help.

Even though things were easing some since the beginning of the Depression, many small farmers like Karl didn't have the extra money to buy the latest cutter and thresher machine: the combine. With Karl's large family, he also couldn't afford to pay the men who would rent out their combine to farmers who had the extra cash on hand to pay for the task.

Karl actually considered use of the threshing machine a time saver. He remembered as a young boy helping his father flailing the small stakes of grain with a flailing stick to get the grain off the stalk after his father had cut it all with a sickle by hand. Now that was backbreaking work. Karl had planted fifty acres of wheat last fall, so there was a large crew to feed during the cutting and threshing.

"Who's all helping?" Rose asked, having overheard her mother and father talking over breakfast the day before the cutting was to start.

Rose's father looked at her perplexed. "The usual."

And when Rose looked as if she didn't get the answer she was looking for, her mother supplied it. "The Ripps will be here, dear, if that's what you're wonderin'."

Rose sighed. She knew that meant Earl was coming as well.

"Your mother's gonna need lots a help today to get ready for tomorrow," Karl said.

Rose nodded her head as she looked down at her lap.

"But if you'd rather help me outside," he said, softening his tone after he caught sight of his daughter's sullen expression,

"I've got to pull the boards and sawhorses out of the barn for the tables this afternoon."

"And tomorrow you can walk dinner out to the field," her mother added.

Rose immediately looked at her mother as if she had suggested she take a stroll across a bed of hot coals. "Oh, no! I couldn't do that!"

Lilly and Karl looked at each other in bewilderment.

"I mean…Mom needs too much help in the kitchen, and I know how much Lilly Mae likes to be outside," she said, throwing out any excuses she could find. "I'll stay and help Mom and Gerty. Katie and Margaret can take Lilly Mae out to the fields. I'm sure Lilly Mae's never seen anyone cut and tie wheat into shocks before. They mostly grow cotton where she grew up.

"What's on the menu anyway, Mom?"

Lilly still hadn't lost the questioning look on her face when she answered her daughter's somewhat unexpected question.

"Well, your sister sacrificed a few of her birds, so we'll be havin' chicken salad sandwiches for dinner. And we've got a fresh ham that I'll put in the oven tomorrow afternoon for supper."

"Well, let's get started then," Rose said, popping out of her seat and reaching for an apron in the narrow kitchen closet.

Both parents looked at each other again and shook their heads.

~ ~ ~

Dinner at the house the next night was at dusk; light was never wasted on idleness. The talk was lively and an occasional cold Pabst could be had by the old and young men alike. Lilly always made sure the children had a special treat, as well, with cold bottles of root beer, orange soda, and ginger ale mixed in with the beer and chunks of ice in the old aluminum wash basin.

The evening meals on each farm the men rotated between were stout affairs and made to show off each family's best in culinary arts and generosity.

Everyman at the long, makeshift table in the Krantz lawn turned as Karl came out of the kitchen with a platter heaping high with thick slices of ham, the sweet smell of cooked pork covered in brown sugar and cloves wafting over the group and silencing them all as he made his way down the length of the table.

Lilly followed with a heaping bowel of her famous celery seed potato salad, the small new potatoes having just been pulled fresh from the garden that morning.

"That looks delicious, Mrs. Krantz!" Earl said as he stood quickly to take the obviously heavy bowl out of her hands. "Silus told me I had to make sure I got some of this."

He set it down on the table covered in a colorful array of lime green, rose, and baby-blue cotton tablecloths.

Earl turned and reached out for the pot of pork and beans that Rose was carrying.

"I can take that," he said.

Rose stopped and stared at him before she spoke. "It's hot," was all she said and walked around him to set it on the table.

"Here's the cabbage salad," Margaret said, stepping up uncomfortably close to the young man.

Earl took one step back. "Thanks." And he took the large, red enameled bowl and handed it to Silus.

Katie brought out a plate with jiggling, cherry Jello sitting precariously on top. She placed it on a smaller table that paralleled the larger one the men were sitting at. This is where the children and women sat.

When all the food had been brought out, Karl stood at the head of the men's table with his fingers resting on the tabletop, and he cleared his throat. The men closest heard his mild attempt at gaining their attention, and they knocked on the man next to them on the bench and pointed silently to Karl. And so it went down the length of the table until the whole bunch was silent, heads bowed.

"Thank you Lord for this bounty, the women who cooked it, and the men who will eat it. Amen."

Then all that could be heard was the clanking of silverware as the men filled their plates to overflowing.

Halfway through the meal, Sam, who was sitting on the other side of Earl, leaned in toward him. "Gotta make sure you leave room for Gerty's pie," he said, as if telling him a closely guarded secret.

But it wasn't a secret; everyone on the work crew knew about Gerty's pies.

"I hope she made rhubarb pie," a man across from Sam said.

"My favorite is cherry," another man said.

"You guys got it all wrong," Silus added, waving his fork as he spoke. "Apple is the best!"

Sam beamed at the pleasant banter about his girlfriend's baking skills.

After dessert and a good half hour of sitting and shooting the bull, both Sam and Earl made a point to bring the dirty dinner dishes into the kitchen where Gerty and Rose were standing at the sink. Gerty accepted each pile of porcelain from Sam with a smile and a final kiss on the cheek. Rose was polite but had little to say.

~ ~ ~

Rose's odd behavior didn't go unnoticed that day. So much so that her parents discussed it as they got ready for bed later that evening.

"Karl, did you notice how Rose didn't say anything to Silus this morning or even at dinner?"

Karl shook his head. "No, but I did notice the looks between her and Earl," he said, attempting to pull the socks off his feet.

It was hard to tell the socks had been white when he had put them on that morning. Now the sweat and grime had stuck them to his feet, and it took Karl some effort to them get off.

"I think they might be sweet on each other," he said with a wry smile. "I told you about what he did for us on the fourth, didn't I?"

"Yes you did, dear, but I'm not so sure about that. She sends letters to that Malcolm fella at least twice a week and gets one back just as often," Lilly said, pulling her nightgown over her head.

Karl was standing in his boxers with a pile of dirty clothes scrunched in his tan, dirt-covered arms when he looked at his wife expectantly.

"I suppose you'll be wantin' some help with your bath water," Lilly said, reading his mind.

Karl walked over and leaned in close to his wife, planting a soft, lingering kiss on her lips.

"The sooner I get clean, the sooner I'll be next to you in bed," he replied with a grin.

Lilly turned her husband toward the door and patted him on the rear, pushing him out of the room. *Yes, and your eyes'll be closed the minute your head hits the pillow*, she thought to herself in amusement.

~ ~ ~

This same scene was played out a week later when the whole crew returned to help with threshing when the wheat had sufficiently dried. This kept Rose in the kitchen and out of sight.

~ ~ ~

Rose decided she couldn't stay for all the remaining things that needed to be done that fall: making sauerkraut and pickles, canning the pork and putting up the corn, tomatoes, and beets, to name a few. She had read something in the paper that August that disturbed her, and she decided she needed to get back to New Orleans and back to school. This was in addition to her growing desire to see Malcolm. Being around Earl was wearing on her, and she ached to hold Malcolm in her arms. She also knew Lilly Mae needed to get back on the riverboat for the fall season.

Lilly Mae was able to stay with Rose for the summer because she was sending money home to her mother. Karl and Lilly had insisted she take some of the egg and berry money after Rose hinted of the sacrifice Lilly Mae was making by staying and helping them out.

Lilly Mae had also decided to take Earl up on his offer of cleaning the movie theatre, once she decided she was going to stay for the summer. She and Rose worked at the movie house every weekend. On Saturday they went in with Karl and Margaret when they sold eggs. On Sundays Rose drove them in after church to clean up from the Saturday features.

"Hurry up Lilly Mae, the library's going to close in fifteen minutes," Rose said as she pulled the trash can down the theatre aisle so Lilly Mae would have something to dump her sweepings into. Rose suddenly froze in place when Earl walked by carrying a box filled with candy for the concession stand.

"He don't say much, do'e," Lilly Mae pointed out.

"That's all right," Rose replied then grabbed the dust pan out of Lilly Mae's hand and held it in front of the pile of debris next to her friend's now-still broom.

The trips to the library each week were very important to Rose. They gave her the opportunity to check out new books, of course, but more importantly, to read the *State Journal*—Madison's daily newspaper.

Madison was the state capitol and thus where the state government was housed, so their paper gave Rose a more detailed view of the larger world around her verses their local rag. She hadn't lost the insight Todd had given her during her stay in St. Louis—how events that took place around the nation and at times even around the world affected everyone. This was particularly true with the impending war in Europe and the present conflict in Asia. It was Rose's job to bring back any news to her father of what Hitler and Mussolini were up to or the latest conquest of the Japanese.

Nineteen-thirty-eight was a tumultuous time. Rose was

getting as concerned as her father about what was going on around the globe. With Michael in flight training in Louisiana, what she was hearing on the radio, what she read in the paper, and what she saw on the occasional movie reel concerned them both. Of course, they were particularly interested in the foreign news. Much to Rose's amazement, her mother seemed to ignore it all.

"Listen to this, Lilly Mae," Rose said as they sat at a table in the library, Rose reading the paper, Lilly Mae engrossed in her latest acquisition on Rose's recommendation, *Gone with the Wind.*

" 'Europe's nerves were taut Saturday night with its worst attack of "war scare jitters" since angry armies faced each other across the German-Czech frontier three months ago....Fuehrer Adolf Hitler's massing of 1,000,000 or more troops for the continent's biggest war maneuvers since the world war beginning Monday, was the chief cause of alarm.' " Rose stopped reading a moment and blankly looked off into nowhere. *This doesn't sound good!* She sighed then continued to read.

" 'Aggravating the tension caused by Germany's ad-mittedly "unusual" war games was a sudden resurgence of Italo-French animosity. This led to a surprise decision by the French government to restrict drastically visits to Italy by Frenchmen, reinforce counter-espionage activities, and bul-wark frontier guards.' "

Then she read farther down the article in silence.

"And here is says that Britain is stopping people from traveling to Germany!"

She put the paper down and looked at Lilly Mae. "This

doesn't sound good, Lilly Mae. I don't care what they say. It all sounds like war to me."

Rose was thinking about a newsreel she had seen in New Orleans that March about the Germans taking over Austria. She wondered who Hitler would be overthrowing next.

"And look at this picture," she said, pointing in disgust to a picture next to the article she was just reading. It showed elderly Jewish men on their knees scrubbing the streets of Vienna as animated Nazi soldiers looked on. "That's just going to make people mad," she continued, shaking her head. "Somebody's going to get pushed too far. They're going to shoot some German, and it's all going to start!"

"That don't mean we're gonna fight," Lilly Mae countered. She had the same opinion as most in the United States at the time—it's not our war.

"Yah, but if the British and French get into it, I can't see how we can stay out."

"You worry too much, Rose," Lilly Mae said, going back to her book.

Out of necessity, Lilly Mae's world was much smaller than Rose's. She had her hands full worrying about what was going on around her. Lilly Mae didn't have the time or the energy to think about what someone else on the other side of the ocean was doing.

Rose *was* more worried lately. She knew if the war started, Michael would be in the thick of things. She also knew she wanted to be a part of it. She wasn't sure what she would do in the service, but she knew she would be there, no matter what.

First, Rose realized, she had to finish high school. And to do that, she had to go back to New Orleans. Or at least that seemed the easiest and made the most sense. She could finish her last year at St. Joseph's, make some money at Madam E.'s, and be close to Malcolm all at the same time. And in the back of her mind it was also a way to get away from the seemingly ever-present Earl. It all seemed to fit. So it was decided. Rose knew she had to leave.

7

Switching Gears

Now, you take care a yourself, Rosie girl," her mother said as she adjusted the collar of her daughter's blouse, a collar that already sat neatly in place. Lilly pursued her lips before she spoke again. "You sure you don't want me to see if they'll take ya at St. Mary's?"

"Mom, we talked about this," Rose said with slight admonition.

"I'm sure they'd welcome a smart girl like you!"

"I have a job that's waiting for me and Malcolm would…"

"Yes, yes, your young man," she said in resignation.

"Well, then drop us a line when you get there so we know ya got back safe."

At that, she pulled Rose up tight, and the two women held each other close.

It was Labor Day weekend, so the small, red train depot in Prairie was bustling. Some of the young adults in the crowd were heading north along the river to the university in LaCrosse or north then west to the Twin Cities to school. Then there were families there who were traveling south to catch a train to the Windy City or were looking to stretch out the warm days of summer in the busy river town of St. Louis. No one took notice of the large, mournful group that huddled around Rose and Lilly Mae.

It wasn't until Rose started sniffling that she and her mother parted. Lilly gave her daughter her handkerchief and blinked away the water from her own eyes. These weren't the first tears Rose had shed. They had actually started the night before. She and Gerty had stayed up late into the night talking as they had their first night together. The tears the night before were mostly tears of joy after Gerty confided in Rose that she was sure Sam would be proposing to her soon. Rose had to promise her sister she would come back for the wedding. There was no question about it, of course, and Rose assured Gerty she would be there and bring Malcolm along with her.

Her father had said a more personal goodbye to Rose that same evening. He had joined her on the edge of the corn field just after dark, while Rose watched the fireflies do their flashing, courtship dance to the cricket's song amongst the tall, dark plants. The feed corn was still standing to allow it to dry before storing it away for the winter, and for some reason, the fireflies seemed attracted to the tall-leafed plants. Watching the fireflies was one of Rose's favorite things on the farm in the late summer and fall, and one of the many things she was already missing.

It was then that Rose realized how she was going to get into the military. It was actually her father who had given her the idea. Karl had thanked Rose for what she had done for her mother those many months ago and suggested that maybe she should become a nurse. He could tell she "had a knack for it."

That was perfect, Rose thought afterwards. *They would need lots of nurses if the war broke out.* She knew it would take her to places she had never seen and put her in situations she could never have dreamt of (and later, she would wish she could stop dreaming of). She had learned growing up on the farm and helping at the Greenwall Medical Clinic in St. Louis that she wasn't squeamish at the sight of blood and was able to keep her calm if someone was hurt. And Rose naively thought being in the military would also help her keep track of her favorite brother. Rose slept that night with a smile on her face and her life neatly mapped out in front of her.

Standing on the deck of the train station, Rose kissed each of her brothers on their foreheads, despite their meager objections, hugged and kissed Katie and Margaret, and held onto small Rachel until the train conductor yelled the familiar "All aboard!"

The awkwardness of being home again had left her the moment her mother had become ill, after which she had little time to think about such things. The only odd thing that never left her were her feelings for Earl, and those she kept locked up tight. This had been eased by her almost weekly letters from Malcolm that were now lovingly tied with a ribbon and tucked away in her suitcase.

Lilly Mae stood stiff amongst the affectionate group.

Gerty stepped up to her and gave her a soft hug. "Thanks for all your help, Lilly Mae."

"Yeah, I really appreciated the help with the chickens," Margaret added after she had given her a hug.

Next in line was Katie. "It was fun havin' you around, Lilly Mae. I hope you come visit again!" she said, sincerely.

She received a lingering embrace from Mrs. Krantz followed by a kiss on the cheek and a heartfelt thank you. Karl gave Lilly Mae a two-handed hand shake and a warm smile.

"You come back and visit, now," he said.

She waved to and got a smile from the boys as they shyly waved back. The boys had come to enjoy Lilly Mae's stories and asked her to repeat them whenever they got the chance.

As Lilly Mae stood looking at the bright faces around her, she realized she would be missing Rose's family and their life on the farm more than she had anticipated. There was just as much work on the farm as on the riverboat, but Lilly Mae thought there was more fun interspersed with the tasks on the Krantz farm. If it weren't for being the only colored in town, she felt she could put down roots in a place like this.

Rose gave Rachel to Gerty, kissed and hugged her parents one last time, picked up their suitcases, and stepped up onto the train behind Lilly Mae, who was struggling with the large care package that Mrs. Krantz had made up for them. It included jellies and jams, canned meat, and canned vegetables, all carefully packed for the trip so the jars wouldn't break. Lilly made sure the package was topped by a large slice of the rhubarb cake Lilly Mae had raved over just the night before at the going-away feast. Mrs. Krantz had felt Lilly Mae was too thin when she had arrived that spring, so once she came home from the hospital, she did her level best to fatten the girl up. Lilly Mae never objected, and she could hardly zip up her skirt for the trip home as a result.

The girls slid into their seat in the train car. Lilly Mae let Rose sit by the window so she could wave goodbye to her family. As Rose sat looking at the group waving enthusiastically at her, she suddenly sat bolt upright, her reciprocal wave slowing to a stop as the smile dissolved from her face. There, running up behind her family, was Earl. He stopped, locked eyes with Rose, and lifted his hand in a gesture of goodbye. Rose raised her hand as well, as the train sluggishly pulled out of the station on its long trip south.

~ ~ ~

Upon their arrival in New Orleans, there were many happy faces at the train station: Madam E. and all her girls were there—Sadie, Ruth, Tess, May, and Jolene. Even Ginny, their cook and laundress, and Millie—Sadie's daughter—came to greet Rose. All eight of Lilly Mae's brothers and sisters stood excitedly on the platform, jumping up and down, trying to get a glimpse of their sister. Lilly Mae's mother was working, so she couldn't be there to greet her. All these eager faces paled in comparison to the earnest young man standing at the edge of the group in a vest and tie with a bouquet of flowers in his hand. Everyone smiled and cooed at the two young lovers as they embraced and melted into a kiss.

"I've missed you so much," Rose whispered in Malcolm's ear as she blinked away the mist from her eyes.

"Why the tears, *Mamsel*?" Malcolm asked, looking into the

bright, blue eyes he was never quite sure he would see again. He had to swallow the lump in his own throat that came at the sight of her.

"It was such a trying summer, Malcolm. You have no idea."

"It must have been hard for ya, your *moman* so ill and all," he said, pulling her in and holding her tight in his arms.

Rose nodded her head in silence.

It took a while for Malcolm to let Rose go, but Rose wanted to hug each one there. Lastly she stepped up to Madam E., who waited patiently on the sideline.

"It's so nice to see you, Rose," Madam E. said. She gave Rose a delicate hug, then held her at arm's length, looking deep into her eyes. The madam tilted her head ever so slightly. "You must be tired, my dear," she said instead of inquiring about the hint of distress she had seen in Rose's eyes. "Let's get you home."

Madam E. put her arm around Rose's shoulder and led her to the waiting cab. Rose let herself be led away from the boisterous group, relieved the madam seemed to understand the jumble of feelings that were overwhelming her at the moment. Malcolm trailed right behind them, Rose's suitcase in hand.

"Just a minute," Rose said, and she turned back toward Lilly Mae who was totally surrounded by her family. They were all excitingly telling Lilly Mae about what had happened over the summer and mostly all at the same time.

Without saying a word, Rose took Lilly Mae in her arms and held her tight. There was so much she needed to say, so much she needed to thank her for, she didn't know where to start. But they were friends, close friends, so all that was said was, "Thank you, Lilly Mae."

Lilly Mae smiled in recognition. She knew what was meant behind those few simple words. They squeezed hands and parted, promising to contact each other soon

~ ~ ~

Rose fell easily back into the routine of the cat house. She donned her school uniform each morning while the girls were asleep, and came home each afternoon to a kitchen full of chattering females eating their breakfast. And at Madam E.'s urging, she even resumed the English lessons for May and Jolene. Japanese being their primary language and the language they still spoke to each other, they still had a long way to go to please the madam.

They had learned a few new words and key phrases while Rose was gone—including some unsavory additions that Sadie and Millie had taught them—but Madam E. knew if they were going to stay in this country, it was best that they learned to read and write as well as speak the language. She wanted to make sure they had a better chance at a decent life when they eventually went out on their own. And more practically for the madam, their foreignness was appealing to her customers. The higher class of men whom Madam E. catered to looked for interesting conversation from their escorts, so in the madam's eyes learning the English language was essential.

Madam E. was happy to get Rose back to her primary job as well: bookkeeping. The madam had put all the receipts and invoices she had accumulated in a box the three months Rose was away, so Rose had a considerable task ahead of her to straightening everything out.

Ginny was also pleased with Rose's return.

"It's good ta have ya back, Rosie girl," Ginny said one afternoon while they were both preparing breakfast for the working girls of the house. She put her arms around Rose and gave her a good squeeze. "Dat boy a yours done a pretty good job fillin' in for ya-all, and he can make a mean pot a jambalya, but he had his own business ta take care a. He couldn't always be around ta help," she said, going back to the sizzling bacon in the frying pan. "And Millie ain't changed in dat department none. Plus she done started school herself."

The place felt like it was back to normal again, for everyone, but most assuredly for Malcolm. Things just didn't seem right for him when Rose was gone. Rose's letters helped some. They kept him up on what she was doing and some of what she was feeling, but in Malcolm's eyes, they were a dim substitute for the real thing. And then there was the continual anxiety over the prospect of her not coming back at all. Malcolm felt this acutely after her mother took ill a second time.

But now he had her with him, and things fell back into their comfortable pattern, with one slight glitch: Rose seemed more somber than normal, a touch out of sorts, and it was obvious to him that she was trying to hide something.

~ ~ ~

It was the third week after Rose had been back that Malcolm decided to find out what this subterfuge was all about. The couple was taking one of their typical evening walks along the Mississippi, making their way west into the garden district to look at the large, flower-laden homes, when Malcolm broached the subject. As an opening gesture he squeezed Rose's hand.

"Are you still worrying about your *moman, cheri*?" he asked in the sweet Creole voice Rose so enjoyed, though the question took some of the song out of his words for Rose.

She hesitated before answering. "Not much," she said. "Actually, I just got a letter from her yesterday. I meant to tell you about it," she quickly followed up. "She said the doctor gave her a clean bill of health, so he's allowing her to slowly return to her normal routine. But I'm not sure my mother knows what slowly means." She chuckled, a slight unease in her voice.

"That's good news!" Malcolm said. Then he hesitated before he continued on. "Maybe there's something at school or at the Ma-dams that's botherin' you?"

"No," she said a bit troubled by his persistence. "Why do you ask?" She felt the warmth starting to rise in her face. *Had Lilly Mae said something to him?* She thought, anxiously.

"Well…you haven't seemed like yourself since you've been back," he replied, measuring his words carefully. "I just thought you might still be worried 'bout your *moman*, or perhaps you missed your *fonmiy*."

Rose eyes widened, but she kept looking straight ahead. She hadn't realized that what, or in this case who, she was having trouble getting off her mind was showing. She had assumed these feelings, these thoughts would just leave her after she had returned to New Orleans and to Malcolm, but they hadn't. And she was troubled to find that she wasn't hiding it as well as she had thought.

"Well, I do miss my family, and I am a little worried about my mother," she told him truthfully, because she did feel these things too. "If her pneumonia came back once, it might come back again."

Rose wanted to fix the notion in Malcolm's mind that her family was the main reason for her somewhat fettered mood. And this was as close to a lie as she was willing to go. Rose knew that her mother was feeling better even before she had left. Lilly had started doing more of her usual work around the house, even though the doctors had not yet given her permission to do so, so Rose could tell she was well on her way to recovery. But Malcolm didn't know that, and Rose knew it was imprudent to tell him otherwise. She wasn't going to let her inability to get Earl off her mind jeopardize her relationship with Malcolm. She knew her idle thoughts of Earl weren't going to lead anywhere. He lived in LaCrosse, and she lived here and that was that. Besides, Rose still cared for Malcolm, and she knew he cared for her just as much, if not more so.

Rose squeezed his hand and gave him a quick peck on the cheek; then they continued to stroll down the street.

"I'm sorry, Malcolm. Going back home was a lot different than I had thought it would be. It felt sort of strange and familiar all at the same time. Then with Mom almost dying right in front of my eyes and..." She stopped herself short, leaving out the other disturbing events she knew were better kept to herself.

But it was sufficient. Malcolm stopped walking and turned Rose to face him. He looked into her eyes and Rose could feel Malcolm's affection and concern pouring over her like warm bath water as he pulled her in close.

Yes, this is what she needed to help her forget. She needed to be held, she needed to be wanted, she needed to be loved. She would forget Earl. It would take some time, but eventually she wouldn't think about him, as least for a long time to come.

~ ~ ~

Gerty was right. Sam did propose to her, but it took until Christmas for him to get up the gumption to do so and then only after Gerty gave him an ultimatum after her twentieth birthday that November had come and gone without a ring. It was decided that the wedding was going to be in November of that next year. It seemed too long to wait for Gerty, but her parents knew that November only made sense when living on a farm. Most everything was taken care of by then—all the crops would be in and the animals would be slaughtered or sold and put up for the season. Everything would be ready for a wedding feast.

Rose was thrilled when she found out she was to be a bridesmaid. Malcolm, on the other hand, wasn't as enamored with the idea. Especially when he realized he would be required to attend the event with her.

By winter the pale that had covered Rose's disposition seemed to have lifted, so Malcolm felt more comfortable entertaining thoughts that they too might get married at some point. Rose would be out of high school that spring, and he was hoping she might be interested in settling down or at least getting engaged. He ultimately concluded that Gerty's wedding would be as good a time as any to meet Rose's family. Plus, he had almost a whole year to prepare himself.

Rose felt more hopeful and amiable herself. Besides the passage of time helping Earl become a distant memory, she fell back into the pleasant attention her happy Creole gave her.

She too had brief inklings of marriage floating in and out of her persistent train of thoughts, spurred by her friends at school or from the bride magazines the women at Madam E. perused. (Even they had dreams of eventually tying the knot.) But Rose's musing had a stipulation. She would consider marriage only after finishing nursing school. She would be a respectable woman of twenty-two by then, and once she had acquired a good job, she could save up some money so they could honeymoon in Europe or maybe even Asia.

May and Jolene frequently told Rose about their homeland, so Rose envisioned herself visiting the port city of Niigata, in West central Japan, where the madam had found the girls—ill treated and half starved—or the smaller village just outside of Niigata where they grew up amid the shacks and rice paddies they so lovingly described.

The other thing that elevated Rose's heart was in September of that same year, Britain and France had signed an appeasement policy with the Germans called the Munich Pact, though it required the two countries to give up much of Czechoslovakia to the Germans to make it work. (Rose wasn't even sure where Czechoslovakia was; she had to look it up on a map.) But Rose was hopeful this would keep the Germans happy and diminish British and French thoughts of war. Most heartening of all was that this would ensure Michael's safety and eliminate her need for going into the service.

Despite this and the objections from both grandmothers, Rose still thought nursing was a good occupation to pursue. "Respectable ladies" didn't take on the vulgar work nurses were required to do—emptying bedpans, seeing body parts that prudent young women just didn't see, let alone talk about.

But Rose agreed with her father, she did have a knack for caring for others. Plus the thought of becoming a teacher or doing office work—the only other two respectable jobs women were allowed to hold away from home—were just too confining to contemplate. Of course, being unemployed was not even an option she let herself consider, even though the girls at Madam E.'s all thought she was crazy. "Stay home and have babies!" they tried to convince her. "Let Malcolm take care of you!" Her mother had told her the very same thing. Rose would have none of it. She didn't have to say too much, however; events soon changed and so would everyone's life for a very long time to come.

~ ~ ~

It started in the spring of that next year—March 1939. Rose was dreaming of her high school graduation. Hitler was dreaming of power. He had taken over the rest of Czechoslovakia, and in April, Benito Mussolini seized Albania—another place Rose had to look up on a map. (Mussolini had already taken over Ethiopia in 1936, something Rose was unaware of until she read about it after his new acquisition that spring.) She had also read in the paper that the war between Japan and China was heating up, and even the Russians were getting into the fray. But those conflicts seemed much farther away. That wasn't a part of the world Rose was concerned about. She was worried her brother would be stationed closer to Europe. Rose knew that the US had closer ties with Europe than with Asia, so like most people in the States, she kept her eyes to the East.

To make matters worse, soon after these unsettling events, Great Britain and France dropped the appeasement pact with

Germany and signed anti-aggression treaties with Turkey, Greece, Romania, and Poland. That same spring Mussolini and Hitler became full allies. These were signs that Rose took as salient. She knew that Mussolini had helped Francisco Franco take over Spain, so now three major countries in Europe were conspiring for who knows what. All these events made Rose eager to get on with graduation and start her nursing education. If a war was going to start, she wanted to be ready for it. It would take her three years to finish nursing school, so she knew she didn't have any time to waste.

Malcolm took the news of Rose's continuing education fairly well. His first reaction was surprise. Marriage and motherhood was what most women Rose's age talked about, so he wasn't sure why Rose wanted to become a nurse. Disappointment soon followed, but when he realized how much this meant to Rose, he knew he didn't have any other choice but to wait for her, again.

Rose spent most of that summer in New Orleans to ease the transition of her imminent absence for both Madam E. and Malcolm, with two weeks at home just before classes were to begin. It didn't seem to matter where she was, however; the summer crept by for Rose until September 5, 1939, the first day of the rest of her life.

8

The Cold, Sandy Ground

he halls of Our Lady of the Lake Hospital in Baton Rouge were all white. They matched the white, silk-seamed stockings, and white shoes that the nurses and student nurses wore alike. The rest of the student nurse's grab consisted of a light-blue, cotton dress that went to the calf, a white apron, and a matching peter-pan collar and cuffs on their short sleeves. The graduated floor nurses and the few remaining private duty nurses were the only ones allowed to wear the crisp, white uniform that identified their rank as full-fledged RNs. There was one other item that distinguished Rose as a student and a novice at The Lake—as it was affectionately called by those who knew it well—it was her lack of the small, starched nurse's cap that everyone who had been on the floor six months or more had earned, and earned it they did.

The uniform was only one of many dictums in the highly restricted, ritualistic, and even militaristic, Christian nursing school Rose had signed up for. Service, obedience, and discipline were the obligatory principles of the French order of the Sisters of Calais—the order that ran the school—and of the nursing programs of the time. These maxims were to be followed whether you were on duty or off. And the needs of the patient superseded even these.

The students were taught by the apprenticeship model of learning: getting their education by some class work but mostly by hands-on experience. This served two purposes. First, it allowed the working staff the experience of the work itself, to teach the student nurses. Second, it helped staff the hospital.

This mode of education was slowly changing, however, as college-educated nurses and professors started to infiltrate the hospital-based nursing programs. Graduate nurses were just starting to be hired by The Lake to educate her students. And RNs were slowly taking over some of the duties that the student nurses had to fill in the past. It wasn't until the class that started in 1940 that this was fully implemented at Our Lady of the Lake. But until that time, Rose's large class of eighteen—seventeen lay women and one French Franciscan nun—were relegated to long hours on the ward and very little sleep if they happened to be manning the night shift. In that case, you were still expected to make it to class the next morning before falling into bed for a much-deserved rest.

The type of uniform a woman wore didn't seem to matter to the doctors, however. They still barked orders at any skirt—blue, white, or black—they caught sight of, and they became even more irritated if those orders weren't immediately obeyed.

It was Rose's second week of her first term, which had her rotating between the day, p.m., and night shifts every month. Rose started on the day shift, which she particularly disliked. That was when the most staff were around, most notably the physicians.

Rose leaned over to Sister Mary Theresa as they were standing together waiting for the head nun to give them their assignments for the day. Sister Mary Theresa was the novice who had come over from France for her nurse's training and, as chance would have it, ended up being Rose's roommate. The head nun had been distracted by a demand by a particular bad tempered physician, so the two young women felt at ease to talk, though only in a whisper.

"I don't think I'll ever get used to the way these doctors talk to the nuns," Rose said in the petite sister's ear. "It just doesn't seem right."

"Zay don't seem to mind," Sister Mary Theresa whispered back in her soft, French accent.

"Well, if they can put up with it, I suppose we can too."

"I sink it is a zob requirement, no?"

Then the girls giggled to themselves, turning a few heads of the other student nurses who glared at the disrespectful pair.

That night Rose made her weekly collect call to Malcolm. He had insisted she call him every week, assuring her that he would pick up the tab.

"So did you do anything on your day off?" Malcolm asked.

"Studied mostly," Rose said.

"That's not much fun when you only get one day off a week."

"I did take a break and took a stroll by the lake."

"That sounds a *little* better," Malcolm said.

Rose sighed. "I still wish you could come up and visit."

"You're the one who told me not to come, that you had too much studying to do," he reminded her. "And you were right, ya know. You need to get yourself dug in there a piece 'fore I come up and start botherin' you."

"Yah, I suppose," Rose agreed, grudgingly.

Even though she had only been at school a couple weeks, she missed Malcolm's almost daily visits when she lived in New Orleans. He always stood so close to her, always wanting to make physical contact in some way, whether it was just the brush of his hip as they stood doing dishes together or the caress of his hand along her arm as he passed her while she practiced English with Mae and Jolene. And then there were his kisses.

Rose sighed. Her body ached for his touch at the mere sound of his voice.

"And besides, you havin' to be in by ten puts a damper on things."

"I know. But if Sister Ann Gabriel catches you coming in late, you get a demerit. And if you get enough of those, you start to lose privileges. Most of the girls aren't willing to risk it and neither am I. We get so few privileges as it is."

"Well, I don't want to be responsible for you losing privileges. I think you'll do that just fine on your own," Malcolm teased.

"Thanks for the vote of confidence!"

Though Rose knew he was right. Rose already spent

more time with patients than the nuns preferred, and she was easily distracted by a patient's request or a job left half done by someone else.

A fellow housemate stepped up behind Rose and tapped her on the shoulder, pointing to the phone.

"I have to go, Malcolm. Helen wants to use the phone."

"But we just got started."

"I know, sweetheart. I'll call you back later if the phone frees up before lights out, but I can't make any promises. Having only one phone in a house full of single women makes it a pretty hot commodity."

"I'll stay at the madam's 'til 10 o'clock, then. Ginny could use a little help, anyway."

"You're a good man, Malcolm." Helen tapped Rose on the shoulder again and bugged her eyes out with impatience. Rose nodded her head in acknowledgement. "I love you, sweetie. I'll write you soon."

But Rose knew the trials she was enduring as a student nurse paled in comparison with the news that was spread across the papers on the first of September. It was Germany's invasion into Poland and the expected declaration of war by Britain and France the following day (along with India, Canada, Australia, New Zealand, and soon after, South Africa). That fall, everyone was glued to the radio or Baton Rouge's local paper—the *Advocate*—to try and figure out what was coming next.

By November, Rose had made good friends of most of her fellow students and in particular Sister Mary Theresa. Rose was enjoying having the French sister as a roommate.

In those rare moments when they were both in their small, austere room together, Rose would try and coax information out of the sister about her native France or learn a bit of the French language.

"Okay, Maragrette, how do you say, 'How are you?' " Rose asked. She had already learned how to say "hello" and "goodbye" and "my name is Rose."

"*Comment allez-vous?*" Sister Mary Theresa said. "And you should really call me Mary Theresa, you know."

"I know, but I like your real name better."

"As a nun, I am to shed my old life and serve only our Lord."

"Like you're shedding your love of cigarettes?" Rose teased.

The small sister gave Rose a crocked smile as she blew smoke out of the open window in their room. Mary Theresa was sitting perched on the window ledge with her nun's veil off, showing off a head of short, dark curls. The young sister was new to the order and was having trouble giving up some of her worldly vices, one being her cigarettes.

Rose's head suddenly turned toward their closed bedroom door.

"I think I hear the sister's rosary!" she whispered as loud as she dared.

Her declaration sent the two women into action; Mary Theresa threw her cigarette out of the window, and the two women worked feverishly to fan any hint of smoke from the room with their pillows and bed covers.

"I did not zink we had inspection on Wednesday?" Mary Theresa lamented.

"Maybe it's a surprise," Rose said. "Helen got caught with food in her room last week, and now she has to repair surgical gloves for a week!"

"Zat's better than Pamula. She has to clean the bloody surgical sponges!"

"What'd she do?" Rose asked, sitting down on the window ledge after being satisfied the room was clear of the smell of cigarettes.

"I zink her uniform was dirty."

"Boy, that's tough. At least she didn't get her day off taken away."

"Or be sent home."

"Yah, they're always threatenin' that one."

They were both silent a moment, listening to the glancing of beads as the sound slowly receded down the hallway.

"So I can really come visit you in Calais?" Rose asked, jumping on her bed.

She had asked this same question for the third day in a row. The young nun had been describing her hometown to Rose and quite innocently had invited her to visit.

The sister shook her head in disbelief. "Yes, yes, as I say before. It is very fine. My family would love to meet you."

"How far is Paris from Calais?"

"By train, not too far," Mary Theresa said. "But it is late, Rose. We need to turn out za lights."

So the women got ready for bed: getting into their nightgowns, brushing their teeth in the shared bathroom down the hall, vigorously brushing their hair out, with Rose planning their vacation together the whole time.

~ ~ ~

With the Thanksgiving holiday just around the corner,

Rose was looking forward to Gerty's wedding and some well-deserved time off. The student nurses didn't have class that week, but they still had the normal shift work at the hospital. Their help was even more acutely needed since the regular staff nurses, who had more seniority, were off at least a few days around the holiday, so Rose was lucky to get the time.

~ ~ ~

Rose giggled to herself at the nervous young man who sat next to her on the train. The closer they got to Wisconsin, the less he sat and the more he paced. He would come and sit by Rose and Lilly Mae periodically, but he always found an excuse to get up and walk about.

Rose was glad she had convinced Lilly Mae to come along to the wedding. It didn't take much coaxing, really. Lilly Mae was tired of the constant motion of riverboat life, and her thoughts and dreams were shifting of late. She was looking to settling down with her beau, Joseph, to a simple life in a small home on the outskirts of the city. She wanted to be close enough to her family and Rose that she could visit when she wanted but far enough away to make a life for herself. But she wasn't going to miss a trip back to a place she considered heaven on Earth. (It had grown in her mind in her absence.)

Lilly Mae hadn't spoke a word most of the trip. She was concentrating on finishing up knitting a sweater—a gift for the groom. She had already knitted a lovely wool purse for the bride. She had procrastinated on the sweater because it was her first attempt at an article of clothing, and it wasn't as easy as she had hoped. She was looking forward to a few hints from

Rose's mother, who was an accomplished knitter, to help her finish it off.

"That boy's gonna wear a hole in dat carpet 'fore he's through," Lilly Mae said without looking up from the work in her lap.

"I know! Isn't it cute!" Rose gushed. She loved how nervous Malcolm was to meet her family. If she had to admit it, she was a little anxious herself. He did have a rather strange occupation, though he made a good living at it. But it was so far removed from life on the farm that her parents and grandparents knew, Rose wasn't sure they would approve. She knew once they met him and he spread on the charm, as he did so easily, even to strangers, they would be pulled in just as she was.

"How'd ya manage to get so many days off?" Lilly Mae asked. "I thought ya said ya only got one day off a week."

"It wasn't easy, that's for sure. I had to agree to work both the Christmas and New Year's holidays before Sister Didease would even consider it. Even though I told her I was in my sister's wedding on the 25th. As it is, I have to work the day shift the morning we get back."

"Same for me," Lilly Mae said. "I has to work the next three weekends at the dry cleaners. Dat ain't gonna leave much time for doing my homework."

"Yah, I meant to ask you how your night classes are coming."

"I only got one real stenography class so far, dat's typin'. First I gots, I mean I *have* ta take stuff like English and math," she said, somewhat discussed. "Don't know why I gots ta… Dang! My teacher said I ain't…There I go again! My teacher says I'm *not gonna* get a job as a stenographer if I don't start talkin' like the white folks do."

"I suppose she's right," Rose replied.

"I done talked dis way for so long…"

"You mean 'I *have* talked this way,'" Rose interrupted her.

"See what I mean! I don't even know I'm doin' it."

The two were silent for a moment, with Lilly Mae tuning back to her knitting and Rose sitting with a furrowed brow.

"I know what we can do!" she said with excitement. "Every time you say something incorrect, I'll tug on my ear like this." Then she pulled down lightly on the lobe of her right ear.

Lilly Mae raised her eyebrows and nodded her head. "Dat'd help," Lilly Mae agreed.

Just then Malcolm walked up to the pair. Rose took his hand when he sat down next to her as they pulled into the station in Dubuque.

"It's not much farther now, sweetheart," Rose tried to reassure him.

But getting closer to most assuredly falling on one's face was not what he wanted to hear. He was trying to understand why meeting these people was such a menacing thought. He usually had an easy time talking to people he didn't know and more so with people he wanted to know; it was one of the reasons he did so well procuring the sometimes-odd objects that people requested. One had to know how to talk with the highbrow and tawdry in society alike to make it in his business. It was the not-so-insignificant fact, of course, that what these people thought of him really mattered to him, because Rose really mattered to him. The idea of anything—and family was a big "anything"—coming between their inevitable joining made it impossible to placate his unnerved mind. So he continued to pace until they finally pulled into the station in Prairie du Chien. At that point,

Malcolm had decided he better calm himself down, or none of this was going to work.

"Very pleased to meet you Mrs. Krantz," was Malcolm's eager reply to Lilly's greeting, after he took off his cap and hastily shook her hand. He immediately turned toward Karl and held out his somewhat sweaty palm. "And Mr. Krantz." He shook Karl's hand firmly. "I'm very happy to finally meet you both! And this must be Rachel," he said with an instantly relaxed smile at the young child in Karl's arms. "Those eyes! Those eyes are the spitin' image of your brother, Michael."

Malcolm's comment riveted Lilly's attention to the young man. *Had he met my son too?* Lilly thought. *Rose hadn't mentioned that.* She made a mental note to ask Rose about that later. It also pleased her that he was able to recognize her children's similarities, traits that were subtle enough that they were insignificant to most men. Rose's mother was instantly intrigued by the young man Rose had talked so much about.

Rose took Malcolm's arm and led him around to meet the rest of her large family. Margaret beamed at the handsome young man. Initially, he tipped his head to her and her sister Katie who was standing by Margaret's side, his hat still in hand. Then when he caught sight of Margaret's expression, he proceeded to greet them as he had done to Rose upon their first encounter—with the majestic bow of a prince to a princess. Katie shrunk at the gesture, a playful smile on her face. Margaret's heart swelled.

Firm handshakes with a comment of "obviously strong men" made the twins grin and take notice, and his crouching on one knee with a question of "who is this intelligent looking young man," made him an instant friend to young John.

Rose beamed at the wonderful first impression he was

making on all of them. He had pulled it off like she hoped he would. Malcolm couldn't see it with the sweat that soaked his collar and made the white shirt under his jacket stick to his skin.

~ ~ ~

"Now, I hope you've saved some room for some of Gerty's famous rhubarb pie, Malcolm." Lilly said.

Malcolm had pushed himself away from the table and leaned back in his chair, stomach distended.

"Oh!" he said surprised, since he had not saved room for much of anything. Then he looked across the table to the sink where Gerty stood. "How could I turn down rhubarb pie!" he said with enthusiasm.

The travelers had missed the main Thanksgiving meal, but there were plenty leftovers for the threesome. Karl had managed to kill two turkeys that fall for the feast to go along with the stuffing, acorn squash, green beans in white sauce, cranberry relish, and fresh mashed potatoes smothered in butter.

"And I know you'll have a piece, Lilly Mae," Rose's mother said setting a hefty slice of the crumble-topped, red and green marvel in front of her.

"Yes, ma'am! Thank you!" she said without looking up.

Along with the serene surroundings and the good company, Lilly Mae had missed the delectable desserts that both Mrs. Krantz and Gerty made on a regular basis.

"Mmm, this is *tres byen*!" Malcolm said with obvious delight. "I don't think I've ever had rhubarb pie."

This revelation surprised Rose's mother, since his genuine

proclamation of interest a moment ago sounded as if he'd had it before.

"*Gran'mar* would love this, if she had the rhubarb to make one!"

"They don't have rhubarb in New Orleans?" Karl asked.

"Not that I know of. And my *Gran'mer* grows every sort of plant that God has on this green earth. She's the local healer in Bishops Parish."

"Your grandmother heals people in your Bishop's church?" Margaret asked in wide-eyed amazement. She hadn't taken her eyes off the handsome, tanned looking young man since he had bowed to her at the railroad station. Margaret was jealous that Rose seemed to attract all the good-looking men.

"No, *cheri*," Malcolm chuckled. "Bishops Parish is a large area west of the city. These areas are much like, I think Rose said you called them counties up here."

"Oh," was all she could say, ignorant of what a county was, as well.

"Bishops Parish is much different than the beautiful hills you have here. It has a beauty all its own," he added with sincerity, settling back in his chair. "A lot of it is bayou and floods in the rainy season. That's why my *Gran'mer's* house is built on stilts."

"You mean it's held up in the air on wood boards?" David questioned.

"Foundations are always stone or block," Sean chided him.

"Well, David actually had it right," Malcolm said.

David looked at his twin with a smug "I told you so" expression.

"All the houses where my *Gran'mer* lives are built off the

ground. It helps keep them dry when the rains come and the bayou flows over its bank. They couldn't be built with stone and mortar 'cause that would fall apart if'in it got wet for too long." Then he paused a moment for emphasis. "It also keeps the crocs outta her bed at night," he said with a smirk on his face, waiting for the boys' reaction.

John responded first. "Your grandma sleeps with a crock?" he asked, quite confused. The only crocks John was familiar with were the large, gray ceramic ones his parents made pickles or sauerkraut in.

His brother Sean was quick to correct him. "No! He means crocodile, dodo."

And at that, Karl reached out without the slightest hesitation and swatted Sean on the back of the head. Sean looked down and pursed his lips tight.

"You mean crocodiles come into your grandma's house!" John said as if nothing had happened.

"Not very often. She usually beats them away with a stick."

Rose rolled her eyes and decided she had better intervene, in case the boys were actually taking Malcolm seriously. "Now, boys, you can't take everything Malcolm says as true," she said, walking up behind him from the sink of dishes with a dishtowel in her hand. "He's been known to stretch the truth a bit."

"Just a little," Lilly Mae added almost in a whisper, in-between bites of pie.

Rose could tell Malcolm had lost his initial inhibitions and was thoroughly enjoying himself telling the boys a few yarns. He was the center of attention, his favorite place to be. But it was getting late, and they had traveled all day. Rose knew he would also enjoy a good night's rest.

"Well, I think the rest of the tall tales will have to wait until tomorrow," Rose announced.

There was a group "Ahh!" around the table as the children slumped in their seats then automatically stood up and shuffled reluctantly out of the room. They knew better not to argue.

"Malcolm, we're going to be puttin' ya on the couch, if you don't mind," Rose's mother explained. "The boys all share a room together, and I don't think you'd be gettin' a lick'a sleep if I put ya in with that crew."

"A mound of hay in the barn would be good enough for me, ma'am," he said as he stood to address her. "I really don't want you to go to any trouble."

"It'll be no trouble a-tall," she said. "We can't be havin' Rose's young man sleepin' with the livestock, now can we. But I best be gettin' up stairs to the boys or no one's gonna be gettin' any sleep tonight."

"I'll help you, Mrs. Krantz!" Lilly Mae offered.

"That'd be mighty sweet of ya, Lilly Mae. I know small Rachel would love to have ya get her ready for the night. Your sweet voice seems to sooth even the most tired young beast!" she said, putting her arm around Lilly Mae as they walked out of the room.

"I better button up the barn," Karl announced as he stood and stepped out of the kitchen door.

With just Gerty, Rose, and himself left in the kitchen, Malcolm saw an opportunity he couldn't pass up. He stepped up next to Gerty and reached for the dishcloth.

"I'll finish up here," he said.

"I…suppose," she stammered. She looked at Rose and,

with a sudden recognition of the situation, she grinned at her sister and handed the wet rag and her apron to Malcolm.

"That wasn't very subtle," Rose smirked after Gerty had left the room.

"I wasn't trying to be subtle, I was trying to get you alone," he said, stepping closer to her to plant a quick peck on her neck as he tied the apron around himself.

Rose instantly hit him playfully with the dishtowel and looked toward the living room to make sure no one had snuck back down to see.

"Stop that!" Rose scolded. Then she turned toward the sink and started drying the clean, wet dishes.

"I can't help it."

He smiled as he dug his hand into the sudsy water.

"Seeing all these dishes makes me want to kiss you."

"And how's that?" Rose asked, incredulous.

And without looking up from what he was doing, he said with candor, "It makes me think of the dishes we might do together someday in our own home."

Rose stopped what she was doing and stared at him, her mouth agape. She had never heard him speak of marriage before. She didn't even know he was thinking about it. Rose thought about marriage on occasion, fleetingly. But she still assumed they wouldn't get married until she was out of nursing school and then only after she had worked at least a year to be able to put some money away. With marriage came the distinct possibility of children, and she wasn't ready for either for a quite awhile.

She went back to drying the dishes without a reply.

"Does that scare you, *cheri*?" Malcolm asked, glancing over at Rose out of the corner of his eye.

"No, it doesn't scare me. It just took me by surprise, is all," she said, keeping her eyes on the dish in her hand and away from his face.

Then she felt a wet, soapy hand take hold of her own. Rose looked up at Malcolm. His face was filled with impetuousness. Rose's was filled with wary. Malcolm pulled her hand to his heart.

"I love you, Rose Marie Krantz, and I want to marry you."

The only sound in the room after that was the sound of breaking porcelain.

"Oh, *mamsel*!" Malcolm exclaimed, and they both bent down to pick up the pieces of the glass saucer on the floor at their feet.

"What happened here?" Karl asked, stepping into the room and seeing the two bent over, picking something off the floor.

"Oh, I just dropped a saucer is all," Rose replied. "Here Malcolm, put the pieces in my apron. I'll take them out to the trash.

"But..." was all Karl could get out before his daughter had streaked across the kitchen and out the door. He couldn't understand why she was taking the broken pieces outside when there was a perfectly good, half empty trash container right there in the kitchen. He just shook his head and chalked it up to another thing he didn't understand about women. Living with a house full of them, he had given up trying to understand them a long time ago.

Karl looked at the young man standing by the sink with the flowery apron around his waist and smiled wistfully.

"Helpin' the little lady out, are ya?" he asked Malcolm

"Oh...yes!" Malcolm chuckled, realizing he was wearing an apron in front of a man who probably would rather swallow a chew of tobacco than wear a woman's article of clothing, let alone one covered in flowers. "I was helping her finish up the dishes."

"Mighty nice of you," Karl replied. He said it in such a way that Malcolm wasn't sure if he was being sincere or sarcastic. "If you're not afraid of getting your hands dirty, I got a tractor wheel I need to take off tomorrow and take to the blacksmith. I could use a hand with that if you're up for it."

"Most assuredly!" Malcolm agreed, standing as straight as he could, trying to fill out his shoulders.

"I'll wake you at six then."

"That'd be fine, sir!"

At that, Karl nodded and headed out of the room.

Malcolm rolled his eyes and leaned on the counter. This wasn't quite the impression he wanted to convey to Rose's father.

~ ~ ~

Rose was oblivious to what was going on in the kitchen just then. She hadn't made it out from behind the barn yet. Her feet seemed to weigh fifty pounds each, and her mind was racing along with her heart.

Was that actually a proposal? Did he really want to get married? She questioned herself for the third or fourth time. *How could he not see how impulsive this was, not to mention imprudent. I can't marry him when I'm in nurse's training, he should know that.* At least she didn't want to. Susan, one of her classmates was married, and the mother superior didn't allow any more than one day and night away from the program a week. And she had to be back promptly at 6:30 the next morning before the seven a.m. shift started.

And what about the war? If the US got into the conflict in Europe, Rose was going to be in it. She couldn't do that if she was married. Didn't he know that? She thought in amazement. *They don't let married women into the service!*

Rose didn't know what to do. She really couldn't fault him for trying to thwart her plans for getting into the military. She hadn't told him about that yet, she hadn't told anyone. She knew he wouldn't approve, so she was waiting for the right time to tell him. But now didn't seem to be the best time for that. Rose didn't know what she was going to say to him, but she realized time was passing as she stood perseverating, and she thought she better get back to the house before he began to worry.

She stepped out from behind the barn and noticed the silhouette of a figure standing on the kitchen porch framed by the light coming from the open door.

"I was getting worried about you, *cheri*," Malcolm said as she stepped up in front of him.

"I...I stopped to pet the kittens," Rose lied.

Then she darted past him and back into the house. Malcolm followed. They met Rose's mother walking into the room, her hands full of linens with a pillow perched on top.

"Here, let me help you with that," Malcolm said, rushing over to her to take the large bundle out of her arms.

"Why thank you, Malcolm," Lilly said. "I was just looking for you two."

"Oh, I broke a dish and took it outside to throw it away," Rose explained as she stepped past her mother.

Lilly looked at the kitchen trash container, which obviously wasn't full, and shook her head in bewilderment. Without lingering on the obvious discrepancy, she went back into the living room to help set up Malcolm's bed. Rose and Malcolm were already doing just that.

Lilly smiled at the young pair working together. It brought back memories of when she and Karl had time to help each other with simple tasks. That was before the children came along, of course. So very long ago.

This Malcolm seems to be a very nice young man, she thought as she watched them. Lilly had noticed that evening how respectful and observant Malcolm was around her daughter. *These things'll be helpful if there's to be a marriage, and they do seem serious enough that that might be a possibility, even soon,* she mused.

Malcolm had also made the effort of coming along to a family wedding, something a young man was not apt to do unless he was at least contemplating serious thoughts. His affection for Rose was obvious to Lilly. She had caught him stealing a glance in Rose's direction or giving her a small touch whenever she got close enough to him. Lilly remembered how that was too— young love. An unexpected smile, a brush of the skin was all it took to feel the excitement of unabashed adoration.

"Thank you, *cheri*," Malcolm said to Rose, catching her hand as she smoothed out the blanket at the foot of the couch. He gave it a squeeze.

"You're welcome," she replied, a somewhat strained smile, Lilly thought, across her face.

"Sleep well, Malcolm," Lilly said to him, surprising the

couple who didn't know she was there. They dropped their joined hands at the sound of her voice.

Lilly waited for Rose at the bottom of the staircase, out of sight of the Malcolm but not out of earshot. She held her daughter around her waist with one arm.

"He seems like a nice young man," she whispered to Rose.

"He is, Mom," Rose whispered back, but with less enthusiasm than Lilly expected.

"Are you tired, dear?"

Rose turned toward her mother without saying a word and wrapped both arms around her. She lingered there in silence before responding, taking in that subtle scent of Lily of the Valley her mother always wore. Rose closed her eyes and sighed. She eventually pulled away from her mother and answered her question quite truthfully, though not fully, Malcolm's proclamation floating ominously just behind her.

"I am tired. It's been a long day!"

Lilly kissed her daughter's forehead and squeezed her hand. "You sleep in in the mornin', Rosie girl. No reason for you to be gettin' up early."

"Thanks, Mom," Rose responded in a weary tone.

Then she clomped up the steps and into bed with the already-snoring Lilly Mae.

~ ~ ~

The next day was filled with activities for everyone. First there was a dress fitting for Rose. The girls' dresses were pink chiffon, with a full, three-quarter length skirt, fitted bodice, short chiffon cape, and matching wide-brimmed hat. Next came meal preparations for the wedding feast the next day—just a family affair at the farm. Finally there was the coiffure consult. Rose, Lilly Mae, the other bridesmaid, and Gerty's best friend, Toots, were trying to find just the right hairstyle for Gerty to go with her veil.

Malcolm was up and done with breakfast before Rose and Lilly Mae even came down stairs. Then it was outside with Karl to help him pull the large, metal tractor tire off the tractor and whatever other jobs Karl could cook up. Malcolm was more than happy to oblige. Even though hard labor was not his usual suit, he did anything Karl asked without so much as a bat of an eye. He wasn't stupid. He knew he was being tested, and he planned on making the grade.

After lunch and a change of clothes, they went over to Grandma O'Leary's and Grandma Krantz's to pick up items for the big event: card tables and chairs, with matching linen tablecloths from Grandma O'Leary—no sawhorse tables for this event—a punch bowl set, wine glasses, glass serving bowls, and a set of silver dinnerware for the wedding party from Grandma Krantz. After they had the items safely stowed away in the truck, they were detained at least an extra half hour at each residence while the grandmothers gave Malcolm the fifth degree along with some sweets: cookies at Grandma O'Leary's and a piece of chocolate cake at Grandmother Krantz's. These tests were even more trying for Malcolm than the physical ones of that morning, but he really didn't mind. He knew what his prize was, and it was worth every drop of sweat, every bite of confection, and every prying question, no matter how veiled.

Rose was pleased that Malcolm was kept busy. It allowed her to skirt her obligation to entertain him when she had plenty of things of her own to do. It also meant she didn't have to be alone with him for any length of time. Rose wasn't up for discussing what had gone on the night before. She was too tired that evening and too busy today to decide what she wanted to do about it.

In fact, they both went to bed that night as the previous night, too exhausted to discuss it, though Malcolm managed to get a rise out of Rose before she went up to her room.

As she finished helping him get his bed ready on the couch, he unexpectedly took her in his arms and swung her around, dipping her low as if on the dance floor. Rose giggled at the boyish grin that was just inches from her face before he kissed her and magically transported her off to another place. This was the man she knew and loved, the man who so easily brought out the love in her.

Rose went to sleep that night in a better frame of mind than the night before, but now with the clear conviction that she would have to have a conversation with Malcolm before long, to set the record straight. Rose liked Malcolm very much. In fact, she really felt that she loved him, but marriage would have to wait, and there would be no arguing the point, at least not in Rose's eyes.

~ ~ ~

The next morning Rose woke even before the rooster crowed, lying in bed watching the sky out her window turn from charcoal to a pale gray. When the rooster finally did sing his early wake-up call, Lilly Mae stirred. Rose saw this as her opportunity to get out of bed and get some coffee going. Most everyone was going to need good, strong coffee this morning. It was the big day, after all.

To Rose's surprise, she heard low voices in the kitchen and the smell of coffee already brewing on the stove as she took her first step down the steep, wooden staircase. Her surprise turned to elation when she caught sight of who was sitting in the kitchen. Malcolm was sitting in his tank undershirt and trousers across from a dapper young man in a khaki military shirt and tie, though the tie was already loosened and hanging to one side, and his green, wool dress coat was sitting on the back of his chair.

Rose ran up to Michael and grabbed him around the neck. He stood with her still clinging to him and hugged her in return.

"Happy to see you too, munchkin!" he joked, his voice strained from the tight hold she had around him.

It took a moment, but Rose finally let go of him. She had felt a weight instantly lift from her shoulders when she caught sight of her big brother. Michael was her confidant, her mentor, and right now, Rose badly needed someone to confide in.

"When did you get in?" Rose asked, excitedly.

"Just about an hour ago. In fact, your friend here was about to take a swing at me with the fire poker before I realized what was going on."

Rose looked at Malcolm with eyes wide.

"I thought he was burglar," he said, shrugging his shoulders. "Who else comes into a home at five in the morning?"

"Well, on a farm, usually it's the farmer!" Michael joked.

"It's so good to see you," Rose mused, a look of relief crossing her face that Michael didn't miss.

"Yes, and your sister Gerty will be very happy with your arrival," Malcolm added.

Malcolm didn't miss Rose's expression either, he just misinterpreted it.

"Gerty was pretty upset when you didn't show up yesterday," Rose said. "Mom had a hard time getting her to stop crying last night. She thought for sure you weren't going to show. She was afraid one of the twins was going to have to take your place as a groomsman!"

"Yeah, I wasn't sure I was going to make it either. It took 'em so long to get my furlough papers through, I missed the train that would have gotten me here yesterday. I had to leave on short notice, so I couldn't call or cable to tell anyone what was going on. But better late than never!" he grinned.

Rose sighed. It *was* better late than never. "You look great, Michael!"

"You look good too, squirt. Hey, sorry I couldn't make it to your graduation party. They had us on maneuvers out in the Gulf until just about a month ago, then I figured there was no use coming down when I'd be seeing you at the wedding, anyway."

"Oh, that's okay," Rose said, sincerely. Rose was proud of graduating from high school, but she saw it as a means to an end. "But I won't forgive you if you miss my nursing graduation."

"Yeah, I was pretty surprised to hear from the folks that you were going to nursing school. I bet the grandmas got their knickers in a knot on that one!"

Rose grinned. "They weren't too pleased with the idea. Most people I tell give me funny look."

Malcolm sat quietly while the two caught up on things, gaily talking as if he wasn't even in the room. At one point, he got a cup and saucer out of the cupboard, poured Rose a cup of coffee, and topped off his and Michael's cups as if he were the host of this gathering. Then he sat back down without saying a word, listening to the two converse.

He could tell even more than the first time they were all together in New Orleans that Michael and Rose had a special bond. Malcolm had already spent a good half hour talking with Michael, getting a less subtle interrogation than he endured at the grandmothers' homes the day before. He could tell Michael wanted to find out about the man his sister was spending so much time with. He understood.

And watching him now, interacting with Rose, Malcolm remembered how being with family always brought out interesting and often different aspects of a person, so he just watched and listened. He was learning all kinds of new things, information he would put away in the mental file he kept to help him piece together the mystery that was his Rose.

Malcolm had already gotten some tidbits from Rose's mother and her younger sisters, things about her surprisingly boyish youth that helped put some of the puzzle together. Now, watching her interact with her oldest brother brought things to light that he had never seen before. With Michael it was a closeness, a reliance that Rose seemed to have with him that Malcolm had never seen in her before. He didn't think Rose relied on anyone, other than herself. This made him feel optimistic. Perhaps, once they were together, she would come to rely on him in this same way, he thought. He smiled at the pleasant idea and continued to take his mental notes.

~ ~ ~

The wedding went off without a hitch. Michael looked like

one of John's wooden soldiers standing up in front of the church in his crisp dress uniform, broad shoulders and expansive chest filling out the fine, green wool to the envy of most of the men in the room and adulation of all of the women. It made Sam's best man pale in comparison in his plain, dark suit and tie. It was hard to tell if Lilly was more proud of her soon-to-be-married daughter or her handsome, patriotic son.

Rose stood a few feet away from the young couple, watching as they stood together in front of the altar and the filled church behind them, her sister in a satin, long-sleeved gown, and Sam in a black suit and tie. Rose thought Gerty looked lovely. The bodice of her dress was form-fitting with a drop waist, coming to a soft point just below her waist. In the back, the skirt spread out and flowed like a thick, milky river three feet behind her down the altar steps. The cream-white fabric was altered only by the forty satin buttons Rose had, moments ago, painstakingly closed and the flowery lace that covered her chest and upper back.

Sam looked handsome in his suit and tie, though a bit like a fish out of water. He fidgeted periodically, and halfway through the mass, Rose noticed a bead of sweat rolled down the side of his face despite the forty-degree temperature outside. Everyone could see and feel the unabashed love that filled them both to overflowing as they held hands and waited patiently for the completion of the ceremony that would make them husband and wife.

As Rose gazed at the loving couple, she felt a slight pang of desire. Watching Gerty and Sam made it easy for Rose to be caught up in the moment and want to be in a similar place with the man she loved. She looked out into the pews and saw Malcolm looking at her with the same wistful visage the wedding couple wore. Rose smiled mildly and turned to accept Gerty's small bouquet of pink roses and baby's breath as she and Sam knelt together on a kneeler put in place just for the wedding couple.

Rose's longing lasted only a moment, however. She reminded herself of her goal. She would be able to wait to wear that gown, to take those vows, to accept that blessing as husband and wife. Rose had other plans and marriage was not one of them, at least not now. She turned her attention back to the proceedings at hand.

The church was filled with family, friends, and neighbors, but it was just immediate family back at the farm for an early supper. The meal was set on three tables in one long line that stretched from the dining room, through a wide arch that separated the two rooms, and into the living room. The feast consisting of both a ham and beef roast, scalloped potatoes, a three-layered, molded Jello salad, preserved sweet corn coated with butter, green beans, and fresh baked rolls, all topped off with home pickled beets, radishes, and dill pickles as relishes.

A wedding cake that Charlotte Ripp, Silus's mother, had made was sitting picturesquely on the kitchen counter waiting to fill in the gaps. Charlotte had taken a cake decorating class in Dubuque that summer and was eager to try out her new skills. Lilly let her give it a try since the price was right—the cost of the ingredients. It had turned out wonderfully. The confection consisted of three, snow-white, tiered layers. Lining the base of each layer were pink tea-rose blossoms flanked by small, green leaves. The top was crowned by a grouping of larger pink roses. Charlotte had also volunteered to help Lilly serve the meal and cut the cake so Lilly could enjoy the event without worrying about every little detail.

The main table was set for the wedding party, parents, and grandmothers. It sparkled with the good dishes, cut wine glasses, and Grandma K's silver. The rest of the adults filled in the two adjoining tables, with the children sitting where they could around the room. Most of the furniture had been either moved to the walls or taken out of the room and set in the barn. It wasn't unusual to have snow and cold in November in Wisconsin, but the room full of chattering guests didn't necessitate getting the fireplace going until well after the relatives had gone home and then everyone was too tired to even bother.

Gerty and Sam were to spend their honeymoon in Chicago, but their wedding night would be at the Hotel Julien in Dubuque.

After the meal and before they cut the cake, Michael caught Rose out on the kitchen porch alone, taking in some of the fresh, cool evening air.

He didn't say anything at first. He just leaned on the porch post while he pulled out a pack of Chesterfield cigarettes, put one in his mouth, cupped his hands around it, and lit it.

"So you gonna tell me what's going on between you and the Cajun?" he said rather nonchalantly, cigarette flipping up and down in his mouth as he spoke. He pulled it out of his mouth, blew out a long wisp of smoke, and waited for Rose's response.

"What do you mean?" Rose replied, not understanding what he was asking, not thinking Michael could actually tell that there was something on her mind.

"Since I been home you seem like you've had something you wanna tell me, and since you haven't told me yet, it can only mean it's got something to do with you and Malcolm," he said, deftly.

Rose looked at him in resignation. She should have realized Michael hadn't lost his touch to read her mind. He seemed to be able to do that with the greatest ease when she was young, and he obviously hadn't lost the skill.

She leaned as casually as she could on the post opposite him, contemplating her response. "I think Malcolm proposed to me the other night," she finally blurted out.

Michael stood erect at the news. "Proposed!" he said, then he hesitated. "What do you mean, you think?"

"Well, we were at the sink doing dishes, and he said something about how doing dishes made him think about how we might do dishes together sometime in our own home."

"Wait a minute! This guy said he wanted to do dishes with you!" He stood silent a moment and shook his head. "Any guy who admits he wants to do dishes has got it bad, for sure!"

"Stop teasing, Michael. This is serious."

"Sorry, Rose. Keep talkin'," he said, composing himself. He leaned back on the porch post and took another drag on his cigarette.

"Well...then he told me he loved me and wanted to marry me."

Michael didn't reply right away. Rose knew then he understood this was serious business.

"What am I gonna do?"

"What do you mean? Don't you love the guy?"

"Of course, I love him, but I can't marry him!"

"Why not? He's got warts in unmentionable places?

"Michael!" she scolded.

"Mom and Dad don't like him?"

"No, that's not it. They like him just fine. It's just that I have to finish nursing school."

"So finish school, then marry the guy."

"But I can't."

"You're losin' me here, Rose," he admitted, obviously confused.

"They won't let you into the service if you're married."

"The service, what do you mean the service?" He said, standing up again, a deep furrow suddenly between his brows.

"With Britain and France in war with Germany and Russia, I know it's only a matter of time before we get pulled in, and I want to be there. I want to do my part. I want to see the world, and I want to keep track of what you're up to, too."

Michael flicked his cigarette out into the lawn then reached over to Rose and grasped her firmly by the shoulders. He looked at her with a seriousness that she had never seen from him before, at least not pointed toward her. "Listen, Rose, from what I hear from the World War I officers in training school, war is no place for women. I don't want you going anywhere near the military."

Rose looked at him with a blank expression on her face. She thought of all the people she knew, Michael would be the last person to tell her she shouldn't join up. Actually, she hadn't told anyone in her family of her plans to join because she suspected no one would accept the idea, with the exception of Michael.

Rose wriggled out of his firm grip and stepped away from him. "Out of everyone, Michael, I thought you would understand the most. You're in the service, why can't I join?"

"It's not the same, Rose."

He looked at his sister's questioning face and knew he had

to be more persuasive than that. "Listen, the men I'm training with are crude; they swear, and spit, and do all kinds of things that aren't fit for a woman's eyes."

"I'm not a buttercup."

It wasn't working yet.

"A soldier has to endure weeks without a bath, three poor meals a day out of a can, every day, seven days a week, going to the bathroom out in the open, not to mention being shot at!"

Rose was silent, a bit more somber. Maybe he was getting to her. He pressed on.

"And what if you're wounded yourself, or taken prisoner?" He was silent a moment, expression draining from his face, thinking of the implication of his own words. "Who knows what they would do to a woman."

He looked at his sister and sighed in relief. He recognized the look of resignation that finally came across her face. Rose looked down at the ground. She was thinking about Michael's words, the risks she would be putting herself into, the difficulties she might face. She had heard what her brother had said. She was old enough to know he was right; these things were real. But what she was thinking wasn't resignation, it was the realization that she wasn't going to be able to tell anyone about her plan. If Michael didn't understand her need to do this, then no one would, not even Malcolm. Maybe especially Malcolm.

"All right, Michael. You win," she said without looking up.

"You know what would be a good idea," he said earnestly. "If you worked in a VA hospital and helped the soldiers once they got home. Now that would be a service to us, Rose. I bet guys wouldn't even complain if a pretty girl like you came at 'em with a six-inch needle!"

Rose smiled timidly, not wanting to give in to him all the way. She knew he wouldn't expect that of her.

"They're out here!" Katie called back into the kitchen after opening the door and finding the two standing on the porch. "We're gonna cut the cake!" she said excitedly to them through the screen.

"Well, we can't miss that!" Michael said in mock enthusiasm. He held open the screen door for his sister and ushered her back into the fray.

9

Marching On

After the big event at the Krantz home, Rose's eyes (and the world's) were turned once more to the East. As nursing school continued for Rose, so did the conquests of Hitler, Mussolini, and now Stalin, who earlier that year had entered the bed of some very strange and dangerous fellows.

The USSR wanted back what it considered its territory in Poland east of the Bug River. Germany wanted to continue its expansion. The German and Russian seizure of Poland that September—a battle that lasted only twenty-eight days— seemed to all like the monumental tragedy it was. Some 200,000 Poles were killed or wounded, along with 40,000 Germans and

3,000 Russians. It gave the Allied forces and the United States alike a very small taste of what was to come. The trench warfare, the very individual battles of "The Great War," were no match for the more modern and deadly German *blitzkrieg*—lightening war. The mobile and destructive tanks, along with the infantry, and the new emphasis on air power that was evident during the Spanish Civil War and was in use by the Japanese against China, was introduced to the whole world anew during these solemn, frightening days that fall. Hitler's propaganda was largely true. They were a force to be reckoned with.

By March of the next year, Russia had bullied Finland into an armistice. June saw the Germans in Denmark and Norway, while their sister country of Sweden, which had also declared neutrality along with them in December the year before, sat untouched. On May 27, 1940 Sister Mary Theresa's precious Calais fell during Hitler's Invasion of the West, which lasted until June and was punctuated by the embarrassing Dunkirk evacuation of some 340,000 British and French troops from the French coast to England. After that great loss, Rose had a hard time convincing Sister Mary not to run home.

"I am glad mamma insisted za family have za gas mask," Sister Mary Theresa said to Rose as she sat red eyed from crying, her half-packed suitcase sitting next to her on her bed. "She says most of za people in town have zem. *Mon Dieu*, zey even have zem for za babies!"

Her crying started a new, and she blew her nose in her handkerchief.

Rose didn't know what to say. She had been reading the *Morning Advocate*, as she did each evening after work while she and Mary Theresa relaxed on their small, narrow beds. She was alerted to the situation in France when she read in a front-page article about the fighting in Europe, "The Germans…already had a foothold at Boulogne and claim another at Calais."

Even though Baton Rouge was not large as most capital cities go—approximately 34,000 in the city and 88,000 in the sprawling suburb of East Baton Rouge Parish—the local paper was a reliable source of war news. In fact, it took many stories straight from the Associated Press. Maybe it was the fact that the stalwart and economically important Baton Rouge company Standard Oil, produced aviation fuel that the local paper kept such close tabs on what was going on overseas. Rose didn't care why the paper did it, she was just glad it did.

Of course, after Rose's vocal exclamation upon reading the article, Mary Theresa insisted on reading the article herself. They both had been keeping closer tabs on the war in Europe after the Germans started their offensive against the Netherlands on May 10, the same day Winston Churchill took office as the new British Prime Minister. Rose had also read in an earlier article about the fear that the Axis powers might consider using poison gas, as had been used with very deadly consequences on both sides during World War I. No one was sure if they would use this despicable form of warfare again, but Rose tried to reassure Sister Mary Theresa nonetheless.

"But they agreed after World War I not to use such things anymore. They wouldn't dare," she said defiantly. Rose put her arm around the small sister and squeezed her gently. "I'm sure your family is all right. You said your father had reinforced your wine cellar. They're probably all down there, safe and sound."

Sister Mary Theresa nodded her head in agreement. She too

wanted to believe what Rose was saying. What else could she do from so far away?

"Besides, the best way to help them now is to get your nursing diploma. We'll both be the most help that way," Rose said to reassure her friend.

She too felt the strong urge to drop everything and leave for Europe. Her brother was investigating the possibility of going overseas to join the RAF—(British) Royal Air Force—while she was stuck here listening to the sisters and doctors in small, stuffy classrooms and tending to the sick and not so sick in the hospital wards.

"Do you plan on going in za war too?" Sister Mary Theresa asked, curious about Rose's stance on the raging debate. The United States as a whole still appeared opposed to entering into the conflict.

"Well, we've been sending stuff over there like crazy after Congress ended the embargo late last year. And the Canadians have sent over troops. Did you know that?"

"No, I did not."

"It's just a matter of time, and we'll be in it right alongside you." Rose said. Then she stood and started to unpack Sister Mary Theresa's suitcase.

"I'm not so sure, Rose. I read papers too," the Sister said, referring to Rose always having her nose in a newspaper or her new source for war news, *Look* magazine. "Zat man in Chicago, who owns za big newspaper zere," Sister Mary Theresa said, struggling to remember his name. Rose filled in the blank.

"Robert McCormick."

"Yes, *Monsieur* McCormick! He tells everyone in his paper

zat you should stay home. Zat it is not your fight," she pointed out. "And za flyer, Lindberg. Many people will listen to him!'

"Most people I talk to think what's going on over there is terrible, Margarette."

Rose closed the lid of the sister's small, cardboard suitcase and slid it under the bed.

"Did I tell you my brother wants to join the Eagle Squadron? You know, the British Air Force," Rose said to lighten the conversation

"No! Do you zink he will do it?"

"I donna know. He's awfully anxious to get in the thick-a-things. He hasn't mentioned anything to my folks yet, though. He doesn't think they'll approve. I think he's right."

"He should stay here where it is safe," Sister Mary Theresa said.

"I couldn't agree with you more, but I can't blame him. He's really doing well in the Air Corps. Did you know he's made second lieutenant?

"Ah, *formidable!*"

"Yah, my mom and dad are pretty proud. We all are, really. But he's frustrated. He's one of the top men in the flight school, but he'd rather be using what he's learned in battle."

"Oh *cher!*" Sister Mary Theresa exclaimed, glancing quickly to her wrist watch "We are to be in class!" The mention of Michael's flight school, reminding them both of their own classes that they, at the moment, were late for.

Rose glanced at the small, round alarm clock sitting on her bedside stand. "Oh, no! That's the third time this month! Sister Ann's gonna take away our day off for sure," Rose lamented and hastily grabbed the small sister's hand, rushing them out of their house and to their inexorable fate.

~ ~ ~

18 May, 1940

Dear Rose,

Things are really happening around here. I don't know if you've heard, but we just finished some major maneuvers. They lasted 2 ½ days and included more than 50 planes and 70,000 men on the ground. The ground operations were undertaken by the "Red Army," out of Texas, and the "Blue Army"—my side— came from Georgia of all places. I wonder if you saw any of the planes flying overhead, or maybe you heard the thousand some army trucks and cars driving through Baton Rouge. I'm sure they used that new bridge of yours that the King Fish built just north of the city. I heard they even brought in the cavalry from Texas. Why they wanted to use horses in this age of modern warfare, I'll never know.

The whole idea was to stop the Reds from taking Alexandria, simulating as close to real battle ground conditions as possible, though I'm not sure you can get the feel for being shot at with real bullets with just tracers in our guns. But it was pretty exciting, anyway, and showed us some things we need to work on. We've run over the exercise so many times now I think I could do it all over again in my sleep. They said there were some 70 generals on hand to monitor the event. Even Ike and General Marshall came by to check it all out.

What was really exciting was all the different aircraft that took part. We had the B17 and A18 bombers, and our fighters, the P-36s. The 27th Bombardment Group's A-24 Dauntless bomber was here, too. (They've been training at our field since February). To help you compare the B17 to the Curtiss P-36, my plane, the Curtiss has a wingspan of 37 ft and has one central 1200hp engine compared to the B17s 103ft wingspan and four 1200hp engines, two on each wing. Our mission was to give the bombers cover for their mock bombing raid on two bridges along the Mississippi, one at Vicksburg and the other in New Orleans. You'll be happy to know we managed "to blow" both bridges! After the bridge operation, our job was to radio in troop positions. This turned out to be very helpful to the guys on the ground.

I got a chance to fly a F2A Buffalo but didn't like the heavy thing much. Someone was thinking when they named that plane; it's about as light and maneuverable as a buffalo with wings! We even had a Hudson here, but I didn't get to fly her. The RAF has been using this bomber since their war began. It's quite a bit smaller than the B17 with a wingspan of 65ft and has 2-1100hp engines, so it's not quite as fast. But I think I would prefer to fly something that size vs the B17. It's a little less of a target!

With all this going on, I'm thinking I might not have to join the RAF after all, though I sure would love to get inside one of those Spitfire fighter planes they fly. They sound like real beauties. Maybe we'll be in this sooner than I thought. Have you heard that Italy attacked Southern France and declared war on the UK? What am I thinking? Of course you did! I know just who to call when the Air Corps wants to know what's going on in Europe. You! Have you ever thought of taking up journalism instead of nursing? You'd be a synch! I wonder if that means the Italians will be in Africa soon fighting the Brits?

I'm sorry those old nuns won't give you any extra time off for your birthday, but I think I can come down for the afternoon. I expect I'll see Malcolm while I'm there! How's the young thief doing, anyway?

They're calling me for mess, so I better get going. I hate to miss the best pile of grits this side of the Mason Dixon line! I'm kidding, of course! Whoever came up with that detestable concoction ought to be shot! I don't mind their biscuits and gravy, but no one can beat a plate of mom's sunny-side-up eggs with a side of our own crisp bacon and that good homemade bread slathered in butter and sweet raspberry jam you girls make. The only thing the bread we get here is good for is rolling up and using as dough balls for catfishing.

See you soon,
Your best big brother,
Michael

~ ~ ~

These events and the fall of France to the Germans in June were also on Malcolm's radar screen. Since Rose would only get one day off a week, and sometimes not even that when time or her mouth got away from her, Malcolm had more of his own time to devote to the gossip of US involvement in the European war. He knew it was inevitable now. And when Congress passed the Naval Expansion Act in July, Malcolm also knew this would be salient for his hometown.

Being at the mouth of the most major inland waterway, and a major port to ocean-going vessels, had always been an advantage to this venerable river town and would soon be again.

Already Malcolm was seeing things leave the ports in greater numbers for the struggling Brits. And the uptick in the number of foreign vessels docked along the river and the industrial canal, he surmised, was most likely due to the fact that the American ships could not carry armaments because of the recent amendment to the Neutrality Act.

While Malcolm bided his time away from Rose, he was occupied, in part, by the growing, upscale subdivision of Lake Vista, on Lake Pontchartrain, and its new residents, with their upscale taste to fill their upscale homes. Malcolm was their man. He knew the ins and outs of his beloved city, and he knew all the right people, on all sides of the tracks. He was able to supply the women who ran these lovely, lakefront homes with just the right chandelier or that must-have vase to be a dazzling accent piece for the grand entrance to their ostentatious homes.

He also had read of the rationing that was going on in Europe—sugar, flour, and gasoline being the main items. And he knew the worse it got over there, the better it got over here for those like himself, who knew how to get things that people needed. Plus the military budget was growing. This, along with Roosevelt's decision to call up the reserves soon after the UK and France declared war, in Malcolm's mind, pointed to one thing. If we ended up in the middle of it all, which looked more and more likely that we would, Malcolm knew he would be in a good place to make some real money—money he could use to buy a home and give Rose the kind of life she deserved.

~ ~ ~

Rose was turning twenty that summer, but she couldn't get

more than a day off the weekend of her birthday, so Malcolm decided to make a big deal of it right at Our Lady of the Lake. It was a nice enough spot for a picnic, he thought.

The four-story hospital got its name in part because it sat on a peninsula on University Lake in Baton Rouge, now much improved from the mule yard that Mother Superior de Bethanie first saw on the site in 1921. The two-story student nurses' house sat just to the north of the Lake hospital building, and there were enough trees to shade the large gathering to make it tolerable on this very hot and humid August afternoon. The nurses' house wasn't air cooled, as the hospital was, so having the party outside was a better choice than in. The water gave a slight cooling effect when the breeze blew just right, though by this time in the year, there was enough dead vegetation in the water to perfume the air with a slight hint of something akin to rotten spinach.

"I can't believe you girls came all the way up here!" Rose said, excited to see the group of well-dressed women standing all around her, the best dressed, of course, being Madam E.

The madam was wearing a short-sleeved, navy, nylon jacket with silver buttons that ran from her white cotton blouse underneath to the white, linen-like nylon skirt that flared out slightly and came to just below her knees, as was the fashion. She topped of the ensemble with a pair of wingtip pumps in white and navy and a white, braided wicker Kerrybrooks hat accented with a navy blue ribbon. The hat looked similar in style to a men's fedora but with a wider brim. You could have plucked her right out of Vogue.

"We didn't figure we'd get struck down in the middle of

the afternoon, even though the place is crawlin' with nuns," Sadie joked.

Madam E. lowered her head almost imperceptibly and narrowed her eyes just enough to make Sadie immediately turn and head for the punch bowl. Sadie's daughter Millie followed close behind. The madam picked up her demure smile and grasped Rose's hand, giving it a slight squeeze.

"We wouldn't have missed this for the world," Madam E. said. "We've missed you so much, my dear. The new girl helps Ginny just fine but doesn't have the head for numbers you do. I have to keep more of an eye on the books than I would like."

"I'm sorry, Madam E. I do miss you-all, too," Rose replied, grasping Bridget's hand. Bridget was standing on the other side of Rose. "The women here are very nice, but we're all so busy we hardly have time to do much together. I spend most of my free time with my roommate, Sister Mary Theresa. I'll introduce you to her. I know you'll love her," Rose said. "She's even teaching me a little French!" she added with excitement.

Rose looked above the heads of the group of mostly women for the petite, brown-eyed young lady in the short, black habit. Rose spied her, ran up and grasped her hand, pulling her over to the meet Madam E. and her girls.

"Mary Theresa, these are the women that I told you about, the ones I used to live within NaOrlins," she said, motioning in their direction. "Okay, let me try the introductions with a little French.

Rose took a deep breath and began. "*Je peux vous présenter* Bridget, *et* May, Jolene, Ruth *et* Tess. Sadie *et la fille*, Millie are *là-bas*," she said, pointing to the colored woman in the oversized pink hat and pink dress with the large, white polka dots. Sadie's daughter, Millie, was standing by her side. Millie's dress, a wine-and-rose-checked play dress covered in daisies, was quite flattering, with its full skirt and fitted, shirred waist. Rose noticed that Millie was turning into a lovely young woman.

"*Très bon*, Rose!"Sister Mary Theresa said, then turned and addressed each woman individually. "*Enchanté*, pleased to meet you," she said, shaking everyone's hand. Each woman nodded and smiled politely.

"*Et voici est* Ginny *et* Miss Edna Dubay, but *Ma-dame préfère* Madam E.," Rose explained.

"Miss Ginny, *Ma-dame*, it is my pleasure to finally meet you all. Rose has talked of you so fondly," she said in her delicate French accent. "Did you know your own St. Francis Sanatorium was za first home to our sisters in your country?" Sister Mary Theresa explained. "Rose, what year was zat?"

"1913."

"Yes! Rose is so good wiz numbers, and I am good wiz names. We make a good team, no?"

"Sure ya do!" Ginny corrected her, not knowing Sister Mary Theresa's "no" really meant "yes."

The small sister looked at Ginny with a questioning glance then pushed it off as the usual linguistical misunderstanding and continued on. "Zey do not give us much free time here, but from za stories Rose tells and what I have read in my books, I would love to come and visit your city before I return...home." The young woman hesitated. "If I have a home to return to," she finished, solemnly.

"Sister Mary Theresa lives in Calais, France," Rose clarified as she put her arm around the small woman's shoulders.

Madam E. stepped up and grasped the sister's hand in both

of hers. "I am so sorry, my dear. But you must tell my about your country," she went on, putting her arm inside the young woman's, then strolling her away from the group. "I have always wanted to visit France."

Rose was always amazed how Madam E. seemed to know just what to say even in the most awkward situations. Rose wished she had that gift. It was usually well after a difficult conversation that Rose would come up with just the right words. It was a perpetual frustration of hers.

As the girls were talking, catching up on all the old gossip, Michael, dressed smartly in his well-pressed, khaki military shirt and tie, strolled over to the group and without Rose noticing, came up behind her and put his hand on her shoulder.

Rose's arms flew up in the air, and she wheeled around so fast that Michael nearly fell over trying to get out of her way.

"Whoa, Rose! It's just me."

"I'm sorry, Michael," she said, somewhat breathless.

"Can't never sneak up on Rose dat way," Ginny said. "Same thing happens ever time."

Michael looked at Rose with consternation. "You never used to be that way."

"I always thought it was somethin' that happened ta her as a chil'," Ginny said.

"No. Not that I'm aware of," Michael said.

Rose smiled and shook her head to try and disarm their concern. "It's nothing. Really!" she said. She grasped her brother comfortably under one arm, ignoring his puzzled look and dexterously moved the attention and the conversation to something else. "Michael, you remember the girls?"

Michael pulled his gaze away from his sister and looked at

the good-looking women standing all around him. "I do, though not as well as some of the other guys," he said, mischievously.

Rose gave him sideways, "not very funny" sort-of glance.

"You girls must be thirsty after your long train ride," Rose said, eager to change the subject once again. "Mary Ellen's made some wonderful punch!"

"I doubt that it's spiked," Ruth whispered in Bridget's ear as they followed Rose and Michael to the glass punch bowl filled with a pink, frothy concoction.

They walked up to the wooden picnic table as another young lady set down a tray full of finger sandwiches made with deviled ham and egg salad. This was to accompany the glass trays of relishes and sweets that already graced the table.

"Eat up before they go bad and we have to pump your stomach!" the young lady jested.

"Hospital humor," Rose explained. "We don't get out much."

"Where's dat beau a yours?" Ginny asked. She was trying to juggle her punch glass in one hand and in the other a plate with two small sandwiches, three sweet pickles, and a couple of white pickled onions, which were rolling perilously toward the edge of her plate.

"I don't know," Rose replied. "He said he had a surprise for me, but that was at least twenty minutes ago. And where did Lilly Mae go off to?"

Just then, from behind the nurse's house came the melodious sound of "When the Saints go Marching In" moving softly across the thick, afternoon air. Soon both Lilly Mae and Malcolm, faces radiant, were seen strutting arm in arm in time to the music. They were leading a four-piece black band as if they were bandleaders in a Mardi Gras parade.

The band consisted of a saxophone, a trumpet, a trombone, and a clarinet, and boy, could those men play! They followed the pompous pair right up to Rose and surrounded her, serenading her with the lively tune.

When they finished, Rose stepped up to Malcolm and Lilly Mae. She was slightly flushed from being put in the spotlight. She kissed Malcolm on the cheek and grasped Lilly Mae's hand tightly.

"What a wonderful surprise!" she squeaked out. "How did you find them?"

"*Cheri*, I thought you knew me better than that." Malcolm smiled a wry smile. "I've got connections."

"Even here?"

"I know a fella in NaOrlans who knows a fella, who told me about...Well, *you* know how it goes."

"I should by now!" Rose chuckled. "You're a regular Huey Long."

"The King Fish? Oh, I'm not that good."

Rose planted another quick peck on his cheek and turned toward the musicians, who started up with the ever-popular "Alexander's Ragtime Band."

The musicians had been playing a mixture of jazz and ragtime for at least a half hour and had only stopped to mop their brows when Malcolm walked out of the nurses' house with a large sheet cake. The band immediately started up the birthday song and everyone joined in. The cake was beautiful, covered in thick, white frosting with three pink roses in each corner and the sentiment "To my Rosebloom – Happy 20th!" written across the top. He set it on the picnic table, beaming from ear to ear.

He cautiously lit the twenty small candles on top of the cake and turned to Rose. "Quick! Make a wish!"

"Malcolm, you shouldn't have! This is all such an extravagance!"

"Anything for my Rose," he replied and planted a small kiss on her cheek.

Rose looked at Malcolm and all the bright faces of her friends, old and new, that surrounded her, and a rush of warmth spread through her body. Rose felt lucky. She had completed her first year of nursing school, and she was doing quite well; she had many friends who cared about her; and she felt very special given the love and affection that Malcolm wrapped her in even from so many miles away. Rose smiled at these thoughts, then gazed down at the small, dancing tongues of yellow-white flame, and a blank expression came across her face.

In the few seconds that Rose stood looking at the candles on top of her cake, a million thoughts ran through her head.

I should wish for an end to the war? was her first thought. It was going so badly for them over there. They had started to bomb England just the month before, and so many people were being killed. It was a sin! But no, this was her birthday. An end to the fighting would be wonderful, but she should wish for something a little more personal.

I should wish for good grades at the end of the summer term, she thought briefly but decided against that too. Rose had breezed through her introduction to nursing, along with her psychology, anatomy, and physiology classes in the first term, though the chemistry and microbiology were more of a challenge.

Her second term was easier, with the almost fifty-fifty split of class time and work on the wards. But fitting in the rest of her classes—sociology, history of nursing, nutrition, food and cookery, and introduction into medical sciences—had been a bit of a trick.

But this next term, her first in year two, she had only six hours in the classroom per week, even less than the nine to ten hours she had that summer. Having less than a quarter of her time in school meant working with patients the majority of the time. This would make her classes in pharmacology, and therapeutics and social problems in nursing that much more meaningful. So making a wish about school would probably be wasted. Besides, a birthday wish should be something more fun than that!

Okay, what I'd really like, what I can't stop thinking about, is to be a nurse, to be a nurse and serve alongside Michael someplace in Europe. That's what I'd really like! Rose closed her eyes, took a deep breath, and blew out all twenty candles in one blow. She wouldn't learn until much later that she would get at least part of her wish.

10

Can't live with'em, can't live without'em

12 *December, 1940*

Dear Rose,

Things continue to be busy here since we started up the flying school about a month ago. The guys that are coming in for training now are getting a shortened version of what I got, but I can't complain too much. They've got me flying tandem with the cadets a good portion of my day. Much better than being stuck in a classroom!

Hey, I heard Sam's number came up! I bet Gerty's pretty upset and probably Mom, too. But maybe it's better this way. Maybe he'll have a better pick at a decent job if he gets in early. Do you know what branch of the service he's going into? Mom didn't say in her last letter.

Speaking of home, are you going to be able to make it home for xmas? I actually wrangled some leave this year. I thought I'd surprise Mom and show up on xmas eve. What better gift than her best son coming home! Though I bet she'd be more interested in seeing you than me.

I wasn't surprised to hear you liked your surgery rotation. I remember you watching dad and I gut out a deer when you were just a small thing, maybe 6 or 7. You wanted to know what all the deer's organs were called. You weren't squeamish one bit. But we had it easy. Our "patient" wasn't supposed to wake up and function after our surgery. Yours are! I'm glad I'm not in your line of work!

Let me know if you're going home and when. Maybe we can hook up on the same train to Yankee territory!

Keep those scalpels sharp!
Your best big brother,
Michael

~ ~ ~

Rose was only able to get two days off around Christmas, not enough time to make it all the way home and back, so she headed south to spend the usual quiet holiday evening at the bordello with Malcolm, Madam E., and the girls. Lilly Mae even managed to stop by for a hot toddy with the solemn group.

There seemed to be a lull in everything, including war news, as the winter set in. But as soon as spring rolled back around, things began heating up in North Africa, and it seemed that the UK was losing the battle of the Atlantic. They would hear almost every day about another British ship that was sunk or hit by those pesky German U-boats somewhere off their Western seaboard or in transit from the States. It seemed a shame to Rose that the US Navy couldn't protect those loaded supply ships a little closer to their destination. Malcolm had explained to her that our boats weren't allowed to go any farther than the mid-Atlantic before they had to turn back. At that point, they handed off the supply convoys to the British. But the British Navy couldn't waste many ships for this type of mission when they were sorely needed for the battles they were waging at home, so the ships weren't as well protected on the second leg of their journey and frequently didn't make it to shore.

Come June, when the big news in the papers was Germany's invasion into Russia, Michael had some big news of his own.

30 June, 1941

Hey Munchkin,

I've got some great news! I've finally been given a real mission! A guy by the name of Rutledge Irvine was here just a couple days ago looking for pilots to go on a special mission. It'll mean giving up my commission in the Air Corps for awhile, but he said once the mission is done, we'd be able to go right back to where we were in the Corps. And the good news is, the money is great: $600/month plus an extra $500 per plane we bring down! That's a far cry from the $120 I'm making now. Of course, I'll *believe it when I see it, but at least it means getting out of here and doing something for once and in a pretty fascinating place!*

I know it sounds too good to be true, but it's legit. When I told my CO I was signing up, he got pretty mad. Schmidty and Al are going, too, so he'll be losing three of his best guys from here, but Mr. Irvine told him he had to let us go. The letter signed by the Naval Secretary Frank Knox and Army General Hab Arnold didn't give him much choice.

I can't tell you where we're going, but I'll give you a hint. Do you remember that book your teacher Miss Turner gave you in 3rd grade, "The Adventures of Little Brother?" I remember it because you made me read it to you almost every night for a month after you got it. Well, I'm going to where that little boy lived.

"China!" Rose said out loud to herself. Rose covered her mouth in disbelief. She did remember that book. It had a yellow cover, and the pictures inside were all black and red, no other colors. The story was about the sometimes-scary adventures of a small boy after he ran away from home and how he made it back home again.

"We're not even at war with the Japanese yet," Rose thought out loud. "Maybe Michael knows something we don't." *That's strange though,* Rose thought. *I thought for sure we'd be fighting in Europe first.* Rose shook her head in confusion, then went back to reading Michael's letter.

Pretty amazing, huh! We're supposed to ship out of San Francisco in July, so I'm taking a week off to head home and say hey to the family before I ship out. I'll stop by and say goodbye to you too. Write me and tell me when you have your next day off. That is if you have any days off in the next month! Try and be extra good, huh. I'd really like to spend a day with you before I go.

And if you think if it, have those sisters say an extra prayer for me. I think I might need it where I'm going. It's not going so good for them I hear.

I'll tell you more when I see you.

Your best big brother,

Michael

~ ~ ~

Rose was looking anxiously among the sea of drab-green, military jackets and hats that clogged the train depot in Baton Rouge. It seemed like everyone in the service was taking leave at the same time. Michael spied Rose first and waved his hat above his head to get her attention.

Rose ran up to her big brother and wrapped her arms around his neck

"Hey there, Munchkin," Michael said.

Rose dropped her embrace then put her arm under his and held on tight. "Oh, Michael. I'm so glad I could see you before you left. I was afraid it wasn't going to work out."

"Well, it was nice of your sister friend to switch days off with you. I wanted to see you too."

"Okay now, you gonna tell me what's going on?" Rose asked, eagerly.

Michael picked up his full duffel bag and flung it easily over his shoulder. "Let's go some place a little less conspicuous,

174

and I'll tell you everything I know. That is, if you can keep a secret!"

Rose grinned slyly.

Michael didn't smile back.

"I'm serious, Rose. This is top-secret stuff. No one's supposed to know what's going on."

Rose's eyes widened in acknowledgment. "Of course. Sorry," Rose said, a bit more subdued. "Let's go back to my room and drop off your bag. I know just the place we can go where we won't be disturbed."

~ ~ ~

The two young people sat quietly on the bench in front of the five-foot, white stone statue of the Virgin Mary. The hospital namesake resided on a small island that was situated about twenty-five yards out into University Lake, attached to land by a wooden pier just wide enough to accommodate two people walking side by side. Rose knew no one would disturb them here. It was the unofficial place that the hospital staff would come when they wanted to be alone. Some liked it as a quiet place for prayer. Others used it when they needed some time away from the seemingly ever-present demands of the sick.

"So how can you be fighting the Japanese when we're not even supposed to be at war with them?" Rose asked.

"That's a good question, squirt. Our main mission is to protect the Burma Road. It's the main supply route for the Chinese in southwest China. If they lose that road, they'd be in tough shape. We don't want the Japanese to have that advantage. The Japs have taken over a lot of the northern territory, so we can't let them have the south too. If China loses to the Japanese, then we're probably next on their list!"

"Wow, I never thought of that."

"Here, look at this," Michael said, pulling out his passport from his breast pocket.

Rose opened it up and saw a clean-cut picture of her handsome brother on the inside dressed in civilian clothes.

"Look at that," he said as he pointed to the line that declared his occupation. Michael smiled from ear to ear.

"Acrobat!" Rose looked shocked at her brother. "You couldn't do a cartwheel to save your soul!"

"Isn't that a hoot! They're false passports, of course. In case we get stopped. They let us pick our occupations. I figured I'm kind of an aerial acrobat. Actually, we've been hired by the Central Aircraft Manufacturing Company of China. Isn't that a mouthful?"

"I'll say!"

"They've hired a hundred American pilots and about twice as many ground crew. We're supposed to be manufacturing, operating, and working on the aircraft over there. That's the official line, anyway. We're really going to be working under a guy by the name of Chennault, Claire Chennault. He's an ex-Air Corps acrobat flier. He taught in flying school too. The official word is that he got hurt and couldn't fly anymore, so he was decommissioned. The gossip is he got the higher ups mad at his flying tactics, and it was highly suggested that he leave the service."

Rose raised her eyebrows at the interesting news.

"Anyway, now he's a colonel in the Chinese Air Force. They say he's the one that had this big idea for the US to get involved over there. I'm kind of anxious to meet the guy. He's supposed to be a pretty amazing flier, no matter what his flying tactics are."

Rose shook her head in amused disbelief, then her face turned serious.

"Have you told Mom and Dad yet?" Rose asked.

"No, I thought this kind of news would be better shared in person. I know Mom's not going to be too pleased."

"Boy, you can say that again. She didn't like you going into the service to begin with. Then when you started training pilots, she thought you'd be safe here, stuck in the states, if we ended up getting into the war."

"Training's okay, but this is going to be wonderful," her brother said, his face lighting up with excitement. "I'm going to China! Think of all the amazing things I'll see. I might even meet Chiang Kai-shek himself! And I'm finally going to be doing what I've been training for all these years! Not to mention the pay's not too shabby."

Rose dropped her eyes. It took her a moment to speak. "I'm worried for you, Michael," was what she finally said. *I wish I were going with you*, was what she really thought.

But Rose still remembered how upset her brother got when she had mentioned that idea to him at Gerty's wedding, so she knew better than to bring it up again.

Michael took her hand out of her lap and held it in his own.

"Listen, Munchkin. I'm sure we're going to be getting into this thing pretty soon, whether it's with the Japs or the Germans. There'll be lots of wounded soldiers coming home that'll need your help," he said, almost reading her mind. "You've only got one more year left, and you'll be able to help out just like me."

He squeezed her hand reassuringly and smiled down at her somber face.

Rose leaned into him, putting her head on his chest. Michael put his arm around his sister. "I really *am* worried about you, Michael."

"I know you are, but I'll be fine. I'm not doing this alone. I'll have a lot of great guys covering my tail."

Michael sighed. He was excited to be going to China, of course, but the prospect was a bit unnerving. He was going to miss having Rose so close by. She was a ready ear when he wanted to take a load off his mind and always an easy laugh. But he knew he had a job to do for his country, and he was more than ready to do his part—at least he hoped he was.

~ ~ ~

Since Michael had left for China in early July, Rose was feeling a little homesick. So when Rose's birthday rolled around again in August of 1941, her parents decided to take a trip south to spend some time with their daughter. It was early enough in the season that the cabbage and the feed corn still had a little ways to go, so Karl felt comfortable enough leaving things in Gerty's capable hands.

Gerty jumped at the chance to move home for a few days and take over running the household while they were gone. Sam had been stationed at Fort Riley, Kansas, after thirteen weeks of boot camp at Fort McCoy in central Wisconsin. This had left her all alone in the small apartment she and Sam rented in downtown Prairie, so Gerty was very bored not having a husband to look after. She had been spending a good portion of her days at the family farm, anyway, to help pass the time.

Before Sam was drafted, he still helped out on his parents' dairy farm, but after they got married, he had nabbed a job at the largest employer in town, the woolen mill. The mill was gearing up because of the new government contracts they had recently acquired for uniforms and military blankets, so they had new job openings, and the work was at a decent rate of pay. Sam couldn't pass it up. Little did Sam know that four months later he would be wearing one of those very same uniforms and sleeping under one of those very same blankets.

"This is a lovely spot, Rosie girl," her mother said, as they strolled arm in arm along the edge of University Lake. Light perspiration covered them both but didn't hinder their desire for close contact. They had left the rest of the small party—Malcolm, Lilly Mae, Lilly Mae's boy friend, Joseph, and Rose's father—to finishing up the rhubarb pie Lilly had cradled in her lap all the way from Wisconsin. She remembered how much Malcolm and Lilly Mae had enjoyed rhubarb on their visit north, and knowing they couldn't get any this far south, she made sure she brought some along.

"Yah, and the river is close by too. I wish we could take more advantage of both, but I still have to find time to study if we're not being asked to work extra hours."

"And how are your studies going?" Lilly asked.

"Just fine. We're in class only six hours a week, but our clinical rotations are where we really learn things anyway. Med-surg was interesting, especially the surgery rotation, but it was hard to switch from that to OB. Pregnant women and infants need such different care then post-op patients. And after seeing my first delivery, I've sworn off having any children," Rose said, adamantly. "I'm not putting myself through that agony. I really don't know how you did it, mom. And nine times, on top of it!"

"Well, they put you under for the worst part, and when you wake up with that beautiful, pink bundle in your arms, all those other things seem to fade away. It must be the good Lord's way of keeping us having children, in addition to givin' men such a healthy appetite for the whole business, if you don't mind me sayin' so."

Rose blushed at her mother's reference.

"Speakin'a men. When's that young man a yours going to be makin' an honest woman outta ya?"

"Mom!" Rose said in a condemning tone.

"Well, you been seeing each other for how long now?

"Four years," she admitted, reluctantly.

"That's plenty a time to know if it's gonna be workin' out between ya. Don't you think?"

"I don't know, Mom."

"It took less than a year with your father and that's only because he was so shy. It was hard to get the man alone long enough to find out what he was really like."

"Marriage is not very practical when I'm in nursing school. Helen's married, and she gets to see her husband maybe once a week—twice if she's able to sneak past Sister Beatrice, and that's not easy! That's not the kind of marriage I want," she said, shaking her head.

"I suppose you're right," her mother admitted, grudgingly. "Lilly Mae's fella seems very nice. I'm glad she brought him along so we could meet him."

"He is very nice, and he really treats her well. As hard as that girl works, she needs a little pampering!"

"You're right about that. I didn't know she was workin' as a stenographer and on the riverboat too! And it sounds like it's only so she can still give her dear mother part of her wages."

"Well, it's that and so she can save up for a place of her own. The two-bedroom apartment that she lives in with her family doesn't give her much privacy. Actually, she'd like me to move in with her once I'm out of nursing school."

"Ahhh, I'm glad you brought that up. Your father and I were wonderin' what your plans were after your trainin'."

Lilly was hoping against hope, of course, that her daughter would finally be coming home, with or without the young man. She'd take her either way.

Rose hesitated a moment and looked down at the mostly brown grass under their feet, the dry blades crunching as they walked along. Since this was her last year of training, she had a strong urge to tell her mother her plans to join the service this next spring. Michael had written her and told her they had three American nurses in his unit. They had come over from a hospital in the Philippines to join the AVG (American Volunteer Group—the name of Michael's outfit). So Rose knew they were sending nurses overseas. Rose didn't expect to get an assignment in China, of course, but she was hoping maybe the Philippines or at least on the island of Hawaii. That way she'd be on the same side of the world as Michael.

She had told Lilly Mae her plans, but in Lilly Mae's usual, practical manner she questioned Rose as to why she would want to travel so far away from home and work in some "God-forsakin' place" where no one spoke "a speck'a English." She was sure Rose would be bit by a snake or swell up from all the mosquito bites and die of some hideous disease. Lilly Mae was a great friend, but she had a hard time seeing past her own circumstances and desires. Rose couldn't really blame her for that, though. Coming from such a large family without a father, Lilly Mae had enough trouble keeping track of her own responsibilities.

Rose sighed and pursed her lips in resolve. As much as she wanted to confide in her mother, she had come to the conclusion that it wouldn't be in anyone's best interest to do so. As upset as her mother was about Michael's going off to China, letting her daughter go so far away would not be acceptable or at least too upsetting to make it worth Rose's desire to tell her mother her plans.

"I'm not really sure, mom," Rose finally lied.

"Well, I know they would jump at the chance to get such a good nurse at Beaumont Hospital."

"I don't..."

But before Rose could finish, her mother cut her off. "I know, I know," Lilly said, putting up her hand to stop her daughter's declination. "Prairie's awfully small for a girl who's been as many places as you have. But you can't blame a mother for trying, now can ya?"

Rose squeezed her mother's arm and smiled. "No, I can't."

The two women walked in silence a few feet before Lilly spoke. "Well, I suppose we outta be gettin' back. They're gonna be thinkin' we fell in the lake and drowned."

Rose chuckled at her mother's dry humor. She knew that's who Michael got it from.

"I suppose," Rose replied.

As the two women headed back toward the birthday gathering, Rose touched her mother's arm and stopped walking.

"I wanted to thank you and dad for coming down here for my birthday, Mom. I didn't want to say anything in front of the others. I know that would embarrass Dad, but I know it's not easy getting away from the farm and the cost of the train and everything..."

"Now don't you be worryin' about it none. We wanted to come."

"Even Daddy?"

"Well, you know your father. It's hard to get him to go anywhere that doesn't involve a piece of farm equipment or some sort of work. But honestly, he's having a wonderful time. I actually think it's gonna be hard ta get him ta leave!"

"I just miss the family so much more since Michael's been gone," Rose said, looking down at the ground.

"I know ya do, dear," her mother said. Lilly took hold of Rose's hand in both of hers. "All the more reason ta start one of your own! That is after ya get married, a course," Lilly said with a resolute expression.

Rose shook her head in admonition. "Mom."

"I could say somethin' to the lad," she kept up.

"Mother!"

"Oh, all right," she said, subjugating to her daughter's condemning stare. She let go of Rose's hand in defeat.

"You're just my next best hope to havin' any grandchildren before they put me six feet under!" Lilly said with a pout. "Poor Gerty and Sam haven't had much luck so far. And with Sam off to Kansas now, those two aren't gonna be givin' me anyone to bounce on my knee for some time ta come."

Rose felt a pang of guilt as her mother spoke. She knew that Malcolm would marry her tomorrow if she gave him any hint of interest in that direction, but Rose was serious about not wanting to be married under such restricted conditions, and since the military didn't take married women, she didn't have much choice. Suddenly Rose thought of a way to make her mother feel better and give Lilly a small thread of hope.

"I tell you what, Mom. Once I graduate, you'll be the first one to know if Malcolm proposes."

Lilly's chest filled and her face brightened at least three-fold. She grasped her daughter around the neck and gave her the strongest hug she had every felt from her mother. Now she knew where she got *that* from.

After letting go of her daughter, not saying a word, she grasped Rose's hand and practically floated the two of them back to the mostly empty pie pan.

⊞ 11 ⊞

A Day that Will Live in Infamy

8 December, 1941

"Mr. Vice President, Mr. Speaker, Members of the Senate and the House of Representatives: Yesterday, December 7th, 1941—a date which will live in infamy—the United States of America was suddenly and deliberately attacked by naval and air forces of the Empire of Japan.

As commander in chief of the Army and Navy, I have

directed that all measures be taken for our defense. But always will our whole nation remember the character of the onslaught against us.

No matter how long it may take us to overcome this premeditated invasion, the American people, in their righteous might, will win through to absolute victory…

I ask that the Congress declare that since the unprovoked and dastardly attack by Japan on Sunday, December 7th, 1941, a state of war has existed between the United States and the Japanese empire."

> Franklin Delano Roosevelt
> President of the United States
> Speech to Congress

~ ~ ~

8 December, 1941

"As soon as I heard last night, that Japan had attached the United States, I felt it necessary that Parliament should be immediately summoned…

It is of the highest importance that there should be no underrating of the gravity of the new dangers we have to meet, either here or in the United States. The enemy has attacked with an audacity which may spring from recklessness, but which may also spring from a conviction of strength. The ordeal to which the English-speaking world and our heroic Russian Allies are being exposed will certainly be hard, especially at the outset, and will probably be long, yet when we look around us over the somber panorama of the world, we have no reason to doubt the justice of our cause or that our strength and will-power will be sufficient to sustain it. We have at least four-fifths of the population of the globe upon our side.

We are responsible for their safety and for their future. In the past we have had a light which flickered, in the present we have a light which flames, and in the future there will be a light which shines over all the land and sea."

> Sir Winston S. Churchill
> Prime Minister of Great Britain
> Speech to the House of Commons

~ ~ ~

If you ask anyone on that day in early December what they were doing when they found out what had happened, they can easily tell you. It was one of those memories that would stick with them forever. It was one of those events.

Of course, back then, they wouldn't know why they would remember it so well—how changed things would all be, how changed *they* would all be after it was over. No one could see that now. How could they? It was an event that would change their world and the world of most everyone on the plant unlike any other event up to and even past this period of time in history. It would create a generation of men and women who, after muddling through the adversity of the depression, would mold their country into something that was much bigger than any of them individually, because that is what they would learn through all the hardship and death: you were only as good as the man or woman next to you, and sometimes your fate was in their hands, just as they all were in God's hands.

If the soldier next to you could step out into the line of fire with just a moment's hesitation, or the parent next door could send their beloved child off to an unknown and often deadly fate with stoic resignation, then you could too. And if you didn't run out and grab your buddy, wounded and moaning on the ground twenty feet away from you, or if you didn't give your meat stamps to the woman two houses down who had three kids to feed while her husband was away, God knows where, then who would?

It was a time of change, a time of banding together for the common good. Opportunities were made: black pilots out of Tuskegee, women working in ammunitions at the Keyport factory in Poulsbo, Washington, and then lost again for some once it was all over.

But things would never be the same. Most people could see that, and those who could, took advantage: Daniel Inouye, a decorated second lieutenant in the 442nd regiment, an all-Japanese American outfit, and future US Senator; Jacqueline Cocharn, leader of the Guinea Pigs, a group of the United States Air Corps Women's Auxiliary Ferrying Squadron (WAFS), who ferried military planes from production facilities to airfields within the United States; Elizabeth Gregory MacGill, the first women aircraft designer working on the Hawker Hurricane and Curtis-Wright Helldriver fighter planes. Concrete examples for all of us, scratched in the history books and etched in the hearts of our elders of what can come from depravity and hardship and pain.

~ ~ ~

They usually didn't allow nurses in the doctor's lounge, but no one was paying attention to that rule this afternoon. Rose was in the middle of her pediatric rotation, making sure the children had everything they needed to drift off to sleep for their afternoon nap.

"Pisst. Rose," came a whisper from behind her as she was tucking in the bed sheets of a particularly reluctant napper. "Rose, come quick!"

Ruthie, a fellow nursing student, was motioning insistently, her eyes wide and compelling.

"I'll be right back, Danny. You try and go to sleep now."

"But I'm not tired," the freckle-faced, strawberry blond insisted.

"I tell you what," Rose whispered to him, leaning in close. "If you just close your eyes and go to sleep, I promise I'll have a surprise for you when you wake up."

"Really?" the small boy said with excitement.

"Really," Rose repeated with a smile, though she didn't know what exactly that surprise would be. She'd figure that out later, or maybe the small boy would forget. No, the children never forgot. After only one week on the pediatric ward, Rose realized they never forgot a promise.

Rose stepped out of the large children's ward but was stopped short when she saw staff trying to be inconspicuous but rushing all the same in the direction of the doctor's lounge at the other end of the hall. *Someone must be hurt!* Rose thought, and she too walked with haste to where the sea of white, light-blue, and black clad bodies were hurrying.

Rose stepped into the lounge and saw the group huddled around the small box radio in absolute silence.

"Wait a minute...yes, yes, it has been officially confirmed; just before 8 a.m. Pacific Standard Time, the Japanese attacked Pearl Harbor on the island of Hawaii. We are only getting sketchy reports on casualties, but it appears our guys were caught completely off guard."

But that was the last Rose heard as the radio continued its chatter. She leaned against the wall for support, her face in a cold stone stare. *Michael!* was all she could think.

"All right, ladies and gentlemen," the floor sister barked out after about five minutes. The voices had started escalating in the small, cramped room. "Time to get back to work. No need to discuss this with patients, is there?" she added. "Come along now. Our patients are waiting." She said this as if she were rousing them from a coffee break.

The staff filed out into the hall, speaking in huddled groups of two and three, or just walking in numbed silence as Rose was doing. Even the doctors blindly followed the sister's orders. Rose walked back into the children's ward and stood staring blankly at the rows of whitewashed, metal beds on each side of the large room.

"Nurse Rose. Nurse Rose," a small voice pulled at Rose's ear. "Nurse Rose!" it said again, more insistent this time.

Rose turned and looked at the small, redheaded boy whom she had tucked into bed just minutes before. It seemed like an eternity.

Rose blinked and brought the small figure into view. She stepped over to the side of Danny's bed and looked down at him, not really registering his face. He looked so small, so innocent, she thought. *Had Michael ever been that small?* He had red hair too, though not as light as this boy's. She only remembered Michael as being big, her big brother—always there for her when she needed him, always there to answer her constant questions when she was small, too small to go to school, and then later always willing to help her with her homework and farm chores. Michael made a point of giving her special attention, or at least that's how it felt to Rose, teasing her or unexpectedly helping her with particularly nasty chores like cleaning out the chicken coup.

Michael hadn't begun any missions yet in China. Rose had gotten a letter from him just this last week. He wrote her long letters at least twice a month since he had made landfall in Burma in late July. But he wasn't in harm's way yet, not exactly. He said that one of the guys in his squadron—they had the funny name, Rose thought, of the "Adam and Eve" squadron had been killed in a training accident that September. The P-40 Hawk Fighters that they were using didn't have any homing gear, and the weather was frequently bad around Rangoon, Burma, where they were training at an RAF airfield. This young man had gotten lost in a monsoon and crash landed somewhere in the Himalayan foothills.

Michael tried to reassure her that Chennault was training them well: Asian geography lessons, Japanese fighter plane tactics, information on the Chinese air-raid warning network, and Chennault's style of aerial fighting tactics. These fighting tactics sounded strange to Michael at first, but during flight practice they worked well with the heavier, less nimble P-40's, compared to the Japanese Zeros that were lighter and had better maneuverability.

But now that would all change. Now they would be flying real missions, against the real enemy, not just protecting a supply line along a precarious, dirt roadway. It wouldn't start in Europe, like she had thought, and Michael would be in the middle of it all. Rose felt very helpless as a tear streaked down the side of her face. She felt a little selfish wishing for her big brother to comfort her, but at the same time, she was very afraid for his life.

Rose was startled out of her morose wanderings by a small, soft hand sliding cautiously into her own. "Are you all right, nurse Rose?" the sweet voice asked.

Rose wiped away the water from her eyes.

"I'm ready for my surprise!" he said eagerly, though with slight trepidation. He could see she was upset.

"Surprise?" Rose was brought back to the expectant face by the odd statement.

"You said you'd give me a surprise if I shut my eyes and took a nap," Danny reminded her with confidence.

"I said that?" Rose said, trying to pull herself back to the earnest voice.

Then she looked at the watch on her wrist and realized the young snipe was trying to pull something over on her.

Her expression changed from bewilderment to wry comprehension. Without a word she lifted his covers up just enough to allow him to lay down in bed easier. "Snuggle down," she ordered gently.

The small boy dropped his shoulders and reluctantly complied.

"I tell you what. I'll sit here and tell you a story until you fall asleep."

"Do I still get my surprise?"

"We're all going to get a surprise," Rose said, solemnly.

When she saw the puzzled look on Danny's face, she revised her statement. "Yes, yes," she reassured him. "You'll get your surprise, but only *after* you take your nap. Now close your eyes." Then she began her story.

"Once upon a time there was a young boy, a boy much younger than you, who lived in the beautiful rolling hills in the Chinese countryside with his sister Water Lilly and their very old grandfather who had a long, white beard." Rose used her hand to pull down on her chin to illustrate the length of the old man's beard. "Water Lilly called this boy Little Brother. He was a special little boy because he actually wasn't a boy at all. He was a doll that Water Lilly's grandfather had made her for their New Year's celebration, but he could dance and sing just like any real live boy."

"Really?" the young boy said, eyes wide with excitement.

"Shhh," Rose said, staring hard at him then shutting her own eyes for him to imitate.

Maybe this wasn't such a good story to tell a youngster she was trying to get to fall asleep, but it was one Rose felt compelled to tell.

Danny pressed his lips together and closed his eyes once more to listen to the story of a China much calmer one than the real one Rose's brother Michael was probably waking up to on the other side of the world.

~ ~ ~

With the US officially in the war, Malcolm's connections were starting to pay off. Military facilities began to spring up seemingly overnight right next to the rich Lake Vista and Lake

Terrace communities along the Southern Pontchartrain shoreline. Even though there was a moratorium on residential building, the military was in full swing, and Malcolm was there to help them get whatever they needed and some of what they didn't.

On the west side of the lake, just east of West End Park, a US Army hospital was going up right next to a Navy hospital and alongside a new Coast Guard station. Farther east a Naval Reserve Aviation Base, an Aircraft Carrier Training Center, and a Rest and Recreation Center soon followed.

The R & R Center was a tent city that was set up for servicemen on leave, so logically both Madam E. and Malcolm knew just what these lonely men needed but the government wasn't allowed to provide. This usually came with a few free passes to the Pontchartrain Beach Amusement Park, which was situated right next door to the R & R Center. Following the lakeshore farther east, the Consolidated Vultee Aircraft Company, the Navy Assembly Plant, and eventually a German POW camp came into being. The Shushan Airport was at the end of military row, and was leased for government use. This was also the site of the US Army Bombing Squadron and Camp Leroy Johnson. All this meant that when Rose's last term and her twenty-second birthday rolled around, Malcolm felt confident and secure in his means to pop the question.

12

Agree to Disagree

"What do you mean, you can't?" Malcolm said with restrained irritation as he stood over a contrite-looking Rose. He had, of course, set up this proposal to be as romantic as any woman could have hoped for. How could she be refusing him?

Rose was in the middle of her last month of training at The Lake, so she did not expect to get any time off for her birthday that year. Malcolm had other plans. He had managed to procure for Mother Henrietta Didesse, the head nun, a particularly expensive piece of x-ray equipment that the Army Hospital in New Orleans had ordered one too many of and that he had volunteered to take off their hands for a very reasonable price.

The discount he gave the squat, rotund sister made him wince at first, but it gave Rose two days off in a row and allowed him to put his plan in motion. It was well worth the price, Malcolm thought at the time. Things had worked out perfectly—that is, up until this moment.

Malcolm started this romantic interlude early, the day before Rose's birthday. That morning he arrived on the red-eye train, sleeping on the two-and-half-hour trip when his excitement let him—in short snatches. He woke Rose (and Sister Mary Theresa) with pebbles at their window and a bouquet of flowers in his hand. He quoted his best Shakespearian love sonnet to what ended up to be almost every nurse in the house as word spread of the early morning bard. It was quite a sight. Malcolm relished the attention from so many attractive young ladies peering out of the windows along with his own true love.

Once Rose was dressed and out the door, they headed for a day of sightseeing, something Rose really hadn't been able to do much in her three years as a nursing student. The young nurses took in the occasional movie or dance downtown but really hadn't seen much beyond the white walls of Our Lady of the Lake Hospital. Malcolm supplied the amorous pair with a light picnic lunch facing the reflecting pools in Victory Park, followed by a short shopping trip down Main Street to Goudehaux's, where Malcolm insisted Rose purchase a lovely, though extravagant, evening dress and matching shoes.

Rose eventually agreed to go along with what she deemed an impractical purchase only after Malcolm acquiesced to her demand that the ensemble would be her birthday and graduation gift all in one.

Rose looked gorgeous. The gown was the deepest aqua-blue, making Rose's already brilliant blue eyes iridescent. The floor-length skirt was made up of small, soft pleats flowing from a wide girdle embroidered in a deeper blue pattern. It flattered Rose's small waist perfectly. The bodice was gathered at the shoulders and crossed in the front to create a soft V-neck. The sleeves were short and only puffy enough to broaden Rose's shoulders a respectable amount.

Rose felt she had probably given in to Malcolm sooner than she should have, but she had never owned something so lovely, and it did seem to be made just for her. It complemented her figure even more than the gown Monty had rented for her the night she and Malcolm had gone out on the town almost four years ago, compliments of Madam E. and the girls. Her figure had filled in since then with more womanly proportions; her hips, now fuller, were a touch wider than her chest; her thighs and calves bore the flawless, muscular curves of a young woman; and her face showed just a hint of maturity, losing its rounder, girlish features, though without a wrinkle in sight. Rose felt like Betty Grable in that dress.

Rose knew something else was up when Malcolm made her put on the new outfit, with the encouragement of the girls in the dorm, while he made himself scarce. When he reappeared in a dapper suit and tie—something Rose had never seen him in before—she knew what he had up his sleeve, and she was prepared for it.

She had practiced the speech she was to give him for weeks now. When he hadn't proposed to her at Christmas, and Valentine's Day went by with only the usual love sonnet and dinner out on the town, she knew he must be planning something for her birthday. And when she heard she had two whole days off, she was prepared for the inevitable. But with the wonderful day Malcolm had made for her so far, she was wavering somewhat in her conviction.

That evening the attractive couple ate at the illustrious Heidelberg Hotel, one of only two skyscrapers in the city other than the state capitol building. At ten stories high, the hotel was small in comparison to the skyscrapers Rose was familiar with in St. Louis; those averaged fifteen stories or more.

Though the food was wonderful, Rose's appetite was squelched at the thought of Malcolm's disappointed face when she would eventually have to turn him down. But when he didn't pop the question at dinner, Rose thought she might be in the clear. That was, until their after-dinner stroll took them to the riverfront and the gangplank of the brightly lit and lively Natchez riverboat.

Rose's stomach tightened as she stepped onto the polished, wooden decking. She tried to get herself to relax and enjoy an evening she would normally have envisioned only in her dreams, but it was no easy task. To her relief, she had managed to do so partially with the help of a few glasses of wine, and the fact that the rest of the evening passed without even an inkling of any kind of proposal.

When the boat pulled out of its slip, the colored band struck up "Moonlight Serenade" as their first tune, just as Malcolm had arranged. It had been their signature dance ever since they had danced to it the night Madam and the girls had set up that special evening for them. Malcolm remembered it well. That night the women, at Madam E.'s request, transformed Rose into the most beautiful thing Malcolm had ever seen. He was glad the madam had suggested he get especially cleaned up himself.

Malcolm had decided, on a whim, to cut his hair short that evening. Prior to that time he had wore it to his shoulders. But he had liked Rose's reaction to his new hairstyle, so he hadn't let it grow any longer since. Malcolm wasn't sure at the time why he had done it, but now, holding Rose close, he remembered why. He had wanted to show Rose that he could be a mature adult, and he wanted to look the part. Tonight was time to take another step into manhood.

When midnight came, a cake appeared, and everyone started singing happy birthday on cue. Malcolm beamed at Rose as the candlelights illuminated and softened the face of his Aphrodite. Rose didn't think anything of his suggestion that they eat their cake out on the bow of the boat. It was warm on the filled dance floor, so she was happy for some fresh river air.

They stepped out to the romantic sight of a crisp, three-quarter moon and its reflection in the still, black water of the Mississippi. The cool river breeze from the lumbering riverboat wisped away the small bit of sweet sweat they were both misted in on this hot August evening. It took Rose a moment to see the perspiring, silver container that held a bottle of champagne along with the two wine glasses that rested on a small, round table in front of them.

~ ~ ~

Rose was sitting now, staring at the champagne-dampened engagement ring that was lying in her palm. She had almost swallowed it. She had not really felt like drinking any more that evening but acquiesced to Malcolm's almost pouting request for the bubbly in order to toast her birthday. He had done so much for her that day. How could she refuse him this? As she tipped the glass to her lips, the moonlight caught the sparkling stone on the ring as it swam in the effervescence. Rose unceremoniously spit the liquor that was in her mouth across the front of Malcolm's suit to avoid swallowing the ring.

She couldn't look into his face right now. She was trying to run her well-rehearsed speech through a somewhat foggy and flustered brain.

"Could you sit down, please? I can't say this with you standing over me, and I don't think I can stand up just now."

Malcolm noisily pulled up a wooden folding chair in front of Rose and plopped himself into it.

Rose looked into his puzzled, questioning face and took a deep breath of the damp, evening air. It helped calm her nerves and sharpen her resolve.

"Malcolm, you must know how much I love you," she started with sincerity.

She had grown to love and care for Malcolm more than she thought she could. She hadn't realized how much he meant to her until she hadn't seen him for over two months the first term of her nurse's training. She remembered the day well. She had finally caught up on her studies and her sleep enough to invite Malcolm up for the day. When she saw him step off the train that morning, her heart jumped in her chest and a wave of comfortable joy came over her that later made her realize the significance he had in her life.

After Rose had finished high school, Malcolm hinted about his interest in getting married. In order to avoid any conflict over the matter, Rose promptly let him know of her plans to start nursing training that fall. Now she had to tell this caring soul that he had to wait even longer, that is, if he wanted to wait at all. Rose knew that was a risk she was taking, but she had to take it.

She set the ring down on her plate, next to the piece of untouched chocolate birthday cake. Malcolm watched her every move. She grasped Malcolm's hand in both of hers. "This day has been more than any girl could have dreamed of, Malcolm. It's been wonderful, and I'll never forget it, but...," Rose hesitated.

"But...?" Malcolm repeated with anticipation.

"But I can't marry you. I've applied with the Red Cross for the Army Nurse Corps."

Malcolm stiffened and sat upright, his face an unidentifiable mask. Rose steadied herself, ready for the torrent.

"What do you mean you can't?"

"I'm sorry, sweetheart. I really am!"

Malcolm stood up in a daze, unconsciously pulling his hand out of hers. He paced back and forth in front of her, lips pursed, eyes in obvious concentration. He stopped in front of Rose after what seemed like hours, stared blankly at her as if she wasn't even there, then began his obvious deliberation again across the shinny decking. Finally he sat back down in front of her, staring at her with a look of resolve.

This time he took Rose's hand in his. "This obviously means a lot to you, *cheri*, or you wouldn't have done this without consulting with me first." He smiled and kissed the soft, white skin on the back of her hand.

"So we get married tomorrow, I mean today! We're dressed for it! You've only a couple weeks left of school. We can live apart for that long," he said. "And when they set you up in some veteran's hospital somewhere, I can come and visit you on weekends. Or if it's not too far away, I'll move, so we can be together. It's not exactly what I had in mind, but if it means that much to you, Rose, then I can manage, for awhile, anyway."

Rose forced a smile at the man who, with grace and forbearance, took news that most men would have never understood let alone acquiesced to. She was more convinced than ever that he loved her. This gave her hope that he would be willing to wait for her again. Unfortunately, she had to tell him what he obviously didn't know.

She looked down at the open tips of her aqua-blue, satin shoes long enough to get up the courage to disappoint him once again. She looked into his loving eyes.

"Malcolm, they don't let married women in the service," she softly replied.

At that statement, Malcolm lost his well-restrained composure. It burst out so loud and so fast that Rose cowered in her chair at an anger she had never seen in him before. It was as if his very face was burning with it.

First he began ranting in Creole, none of which Rose understood, of course. Then, when his temper cooled slightly, he spoke of the various sacrifices he had made for her over the years.

"Does it mean nothing that I had spent my whole summer filling in for you at the madam's, forgoing my own business while you were back home nursing your mother back to health."

"Of course..." Rose tried to say, but he cut her off.

"I am not done talking!" he blurted out fiercely then started pacing again. "And when you came back, something had happened up there that you weren't willing to tell me, something you obviously couldn't tell me, so I knew it had nothing to do with your mother or her illness. Do you think me a *kouiyon*?"

Rose's body sank perceivably into her chair. She had no idea what a *kouiyon* was, but it didn't sound good.

Malcolm looked down at her in silence before he went on, his fierce brown eyes painfully burrowing into her. Was he doing that for emphasis, or waiting for Rose to contradict him? She couldn't tell, but she was too frightened to say a word.

"Then there was this hare-brained idea of yours to go to nursing school. We could have married then, started a family."

He sat down in front of her, trying to relax his voice as he spoke further. He was running out of steam.

"I know I wasn't making much back then, *cheri*, but we would have gotten by."

Rose stared at him but stayed mute. Malcolm dropped against the back in his chair as if pushed by a physical blow.

"After finding out how important it was to you, I decided you might as well go. And I did need time to get my finances in better shape too. So I put up with seeing you twice maybe three times each term for three years, Rose. *Twa lonnens*!" he said, holding up three fingers in front of her. "That wasn't easy."

"I know," Rose admitted somberly.

"Then with the war starting in Europe, and now that we're in it, well, you know how well things are going for me."

Malcolm leaned forward again and took hold of Rose's hand once more, anticipation written all over him.

"We could get a nice place in the city or in a parish on the edge of town, if that suits you better. You could work at St. Francis or maybe one of the military hospitals if you want to work with the servicemen, then I can keep things going with the military installations. We'd do just fine, *cheri*, just fine." His face was pleading now, his hopes and dreams laid and exposed in her lap.

Rose lowered her eyes and spoke without looking up. "It's not just that I want to work with servicemen, Malcolm." She forced herself to look up at him. "I want to be in the service, to do my part, to travel overseas."

Malcolm pulled away as a look of understanding and sour disappointment came over him.

"Ah, *mo konpronn*! That is why you want this so bad; you want to see all those foreign places you're always reading about."

Malcolm started to pace again, his arms gesticulating randomly as he spoke. "I thought that travel bug might leave you once you got your nursing diploma. I thought once you saw how well I was doing, you would see what a nice life we could have together right here in Louisiana. I'd even make enough money for a couple trips back to Wisconsin each year. Then the babies would come, and we could settle down to a quiet life together."

He dropped into his chair, deflated and talked out.

"But Malcolm," Rose interjected. "With things the way they are in Europe and the Pacific, it's probably just a matter of time before your number comes up."

Malcolm looked at her almost as if she had slapped him in the face, then he dropped his gaze.

"It already has," he said almost in a whisper.

Rose sat bolt upright. "What did you say?"

"I said, it already has," he said with more conviction.

"Oh sweetheart, why didn't you tell me?" Rose said with

great concern, holding onto his forearm, trying to get him to look at her. "When do you have to go?"

She instantly forgot all about their argument. This changed everything in Rose's eyes. This was even better. Now he could hardly refuse her desire to join the military. Now they would be defending their country together. Rose felt heartened at the prospect.

He stood and walked over to the white, boat rail. He leaned on it and looked toward the hundreds of small lights of the Standard Oil Company and city just beyond that twinkled and illuminated the haze in the sky over Baton Rouge.

Rose sensed his anxiety and stood up next to him, threading her arm in his and looking at the silhouette of his handsome face, with its broad forehead, slightly enlarged nose, and strong, square chin against the moonlit black of night. He still didn't look at her when he finally spoke.

"I got a deferment, Rose."

Rose pulled away from him in surprise.

"A deferment?" she said annoyed and confused all at once.

Malcolm continued talking as he gazed toward shore.

"The Army was pretty anxious to get their new hospital up and running, so I pulled some stings, got some materials they needed just at the right time, and hooked them up with the best contractors in NaOrlins. So when my number came up, I just cashed in my chips," he said matter-of-factly, then he turned slowly to face her.

"So you don't have to go?"

Rose was still unsure of what he was saying.

"I suggested that maybe I was more useful to them here

than on some God-forsaken jungle island in the Pacific, so they gave me a deferment."

"But it's your duty!"

Rose looked at him puzzled. *How could Malcolm have done this? How could he even consider not fighting for his country?* Rose had read in the paper about the Japanese sub that had surfaced off the coast of Santa Barbara, California, that February and shot up an oilrig. Isn't that why they were interning Japanese-Americans? (Though Rose wasn't entirely comfortable with this policy, she decided the government knew best. And besides, who knew what the Japanese would do next or who they would use to carry out their plans. This was serious business.)

Rose had been a bit disappointed with Malcolm, anyway, when he didn't enlist on his own after they attacked Pearl Harbor—over three thousand men lost and eighteen ships sunk or damaged. If she could have, she would have enlisted on the spot. But with only two terms left in her nurse's training, it didn't make sense not to get her diploma. Rose knew she'd be more useful to any branch of the service as a full-fledged nurse.

And what about Michael? Rose had gotten a letter from him at the beginning of August dated one month earlier. He shocked Rose by telling her that as of July 4, they had flown their last mission as *fei-her*—Flying Tigers—the name given to them by a Chinese newspaper for the sharks teeth they painted on the front of the P-40 Tomahawk airplanes they flew. He was so proud that they had shot down five enemy fighters that day, and a group of them had escorted US Army Air Corps B-24s to bomb an air base at Canton. That added to their record of 292 downed Japanese planes. Rose was glad to hear the news.

But Michael was unsure of what he wanted to do next. He wasn't considered an ace yet; he had only shot down three out of the five planes needed for that distinction. And it sounded like he had gotten accustomed to the dry, dusty conditions at Kunming airfield, where the AVGs 1st Squadron was based, but he did admit to feeling a little homesick. He also said something strange in his letter that had puzzled Rose.

Stillwell (we affectionately call him "Vinegar Joe") brought in General Bissell to try and convince us all to stay. He told us that if we didn't want to join the CATF (China Air Task Force) we would have to pay our own way back home. He also threatened us by saying we'd be picked up at any US port we ended up at and drafted into the army as infantry. How's that for sweet talk!

One of the other AVG pilots Michael called "Tex" had convinced him and about twenty-five other pilots to stay on at least two more weeks to help break in the new crew, so that was what he was going to do. Rose was worried for her brother, but she knew he wouldn't give up flying. Whether it was in China or in Europe, he would be in harm's way no matter where he ended up.

Rose was vexed. How could Malcolm not want to support Michael, even though she realized he probably wouldn't be fighting right next to him? But who knows, he could be assigned to one of the carriers like the *USS Enterprise* or *USS Hornet* that had survived that wonderfully fought battle of Midway that Rose had read about in *Look* magazine that July or those brave men who followed Colonel James Doolittle on their risky raid on the island of Japan. He could even be stationed here at home defending our coasts! Rose was lost in her thoughts, looking down into the coal-black waters of the Mississippi, when Malcolm grasped Rose by both arms to get her attention. He looked straight into her eyes.

"But don't you understand, *mo laime*? If I stay here, we will be set in no time. I can make enough money to put us up in a nice bungalow in a quiet parish on the outskirts of the city, maybe even in Lake Vista!"

He could tell from the puckered expression on her face that this wasn't working. Didn't she understand how this was a once-in-a-lifetime opportunity for a man like him. He had to "catch as catch can," as he had heard his father say so many times. But his desires weren't all self-serving; he cared about his country too. He cared about it more than Rose could ever know. It had given him and many generations of his family the freedoms and choices they could never have gotten in The Dominque—the birthplace of his great, great, great grandmother. Malcolm wasn't sure where her husband was from. The family rumor was that he was French, and Malcolm liked that idea, so he took it as truth. The freedoms his relatives had acquired in this new land translated for them, as well as for himself, as opportunities and gave them the relative flexibility to live the kind of lifestyle he had grown up with—relaxed and on his own terms. This meant, up until recently, that he made enough just to get by.

There were still many people he knew that were just making ends meet. The rich families he worked for in Lake Vista were the exception, not the rule. The main thrust of the Depression may have been over, but it didn't leave many families with much. Then with the war on and things starting to get tighter again, he didn't see the situation improving for some time to come. The military was spending money, but only a few got in on that initial wave. The workers that were close enough to the manufacturing plants to get the new jobs were doing okay, that is, if there were new jobs to be had. Some new positions had been created, but most just changed gears, so to speak. Where they were once building sleek new roadsters, now they made jeeps, or military planes; where they normally pressed aluminum into cake pans and jello molds, now they manufactured canteens and shell boxes.

But the war was raging on as Malcolm and Rose made their separate plans, and there were fewer and fewer men to work in the states. Operation Torch, set for November, would send over six hundred ships carrying some one hundred thousand American men across the Atlantic to join Major Montgomery's forces, striking the Vichy French and eventually Rommel's German troops in North Africa.

And in the Pacific theater things were not going well. The Philippines was lost on May 6 with more than 79,000 American and Filipino men, and seventy-seven nurses, captured. The battle for the Dutch East Indies hadn't gone well, either, and they were still fighting in the Solomon Islands. The men on Guadalcanal always seemed to be fighting the Japanese for the precious Henderson Airfield in the middle of a mosquito-infested mud bath, while men fought in New Guinea almost to the end of the war. Hundreds of thousands of men had been sent to strange-sounding places a long way from home.

As the men started to leave in droves for basic training, most companies working for the war effort didn't have much choice, they had to hire women and blacks or they would have to shut down at a time when it was critical for the war effort to remain open. But even if a woman or a colored took a man's place on the shop floor, they were paid less than the men they replaced. This didn't put much extra into their wallets and subsequently didn't pump much back into the economy. Then when rationing started in May 1942, it took quite a few stamps to get your allotted four gallons of gas for the average Joe, ten pounds of sugar, or even a couple pounds of butter for a family of four. And things were only starting to get rough in the States.

If Malcolm was anything, he was a pragmatist. He kept track of what was happening on the war front as much as Rose did, and he knew things were going to get worse before they got better. America's allies were making a little headway in Africa, but there was a long way to go to free most of Europe and the Pacific. So for an opportunist like himself, all this meant work, money, and ultimately security for him and, more importantly in Malcolm's eyes, for his as-yet formed family.

He also knew that his own family had nothing to offer him other than a pat on the back and a few encouraging words. He needed to make money where and when he could. This war was that opportunity, and he couldn't, no wouldn't, pass it up. He needed this to support Rose and the family he hoped would soon follow their marriage, but now even that looked in jeopardy. He had to make her understand. Rose spoke before he could form the right words.

"This isn't about us, Malcolm. Our country needs us. You've read the paper about how poorly the British are doing against the Germans in Africa. My guess is Africa's the next place they're going to be sending our troops. And what about the German secret agents that were found in Florida and New York or the boats that have been torpedoed right off our own shores? How can you ignore things like that and go about your own business?"

"But my business *will* help the war effort, don't you see?" he said almost pleading for understanding. "I know things and can do things for these new military installations that no one else can. This is my town. These are my people."

"Your business mostly helps *you!*" Rose shot back.

Malcolm looked at her and stared, his mouth open in disbelief. She wasn't getting it. She wasn't going to get it. It was then Malcolm decided he shouldn't try and press his position any longer. It would just upset her more and that wasn't part of his plan for the evening.

Rose didn't understand the responsibility that a man had to look after and supply for his family. How could she; she was a woman. All women had to worry about was what clothes the kids would wear and what to make for dinner each night when her husband got home from work. It wasn't her responsibility to fend for the family. And Malcolm didn't want to just get by. He wanted to give his family more than he'd had. His kids would finish high school for sure. He would see to that. Maybe they could even go onto college or join a trade. Malcolm wasn't able to go past the ninth grade himself. He had to get a job after his father left him and his grandmother alone.

His grandmother didn't have much money. She was the local healer, and the poor Cajun people he grew up around rarely paid her in money. It was a chicken here or batch of shrimp there, and on occasion a goat that gave milk, but many times only a hug and a promise of more when "things turned 'round." So Malcolm knew he had to pull his own weight.

But his father did leave him with some skills.

When Malcolm was still in grade school, he would follow his father into the city during his summers off. He would help him with the many odd jobs that took him to all parts of the city, rich and poor. Malcolm watched him carefully and learned how to interact with the myriad people they came in contact with. And as the years passed, Malcolm realized he had his father's same gift, the gift of being able to talk easily with any one of any class and get most anything from them he needed or wanted.

New Orleans was an old community. There was a plethora of old money in that town if you knew where to look. If Malcolm's father had taught him anything, he had taught him how to spot money: old money, new money, and everything in between, even though once his father had it, he couldn't seem to keep it from flowing through his fingers, either with failed business schemes or down his throat as he drowned in his seemingly ever-present melancholy.

So Malcolm knew it was in Rose's best interest that he stay home and use his skills and contacts to their advantage, but she didn't understand that, and it seemed he wasn't going to persuade her any different.

Rose shook her head in disbelief. After their many years together, Rose wasn't sure she really knew this man. How could he think only about his own bank account at a time like this even if it was for the both of them? At this moment, she wasn't so sure if she was even free to marry him that she would. Rose was seeing a side of Malcolm she didn't approve of.

Malcolm finally spoke. "Anyway, this conversation isn't about me, it's about us," he said, trying to gently steer the discussion back to his original proposition.

"I can't marry you, Malcolm. I'm going into the service

and that is all there is to it," she stated with renewed conviction. "If you can't see why that's important, then I guess we're done talking."

"Maybe that's best," Malcolm admitted. He didn't want the entire evening ruined, even if she was rejecting his proposal.

Rose picked up the shiny silver ring off her cake plate and looked at it. It was a lovely ring: a one-eighth-carat diamond in a delicate filigree setting. It matched the heart he had given her those many Christmases ago. Reflexively Rose reached up and touched the necklace as she remembered that romantic night. Malcolm knew she would love the ring, and she did.

Rose sighed and handed it tentatively back to him. At twenty-two, she was at her prime for getting married. Most of the girls in her nursing class were just waiting to get out of school and get hitched. In fact, five of them were already engaged. Rose was going to catch heck when word got around that she had said no to Malcolm's offer of marriage, an offer that was done in the usual Malcolm style—well thought-out and with great panache.

"I'm sorry, Malcolm," Rose said in a contrite tone, handing him the ring.

"I'm sorry too," he replied as he put the ring back in his breast pocket.

Malcolm stood staring at Rose. Maybe this war would be over faster than he thought. Maybe she would be assigned to a military hospital in Louisiana. Maybe Rose would get in and discover it wasn't what she wanted after all, and then they could be married.

Those were a lot of maybes coursing through Malcolm's brain, and he knew it. But right now, that was all he had to hang onto. He didn't even want to think of the maybes associated with anything that had to do with Rose getting hurt in all this mess or even killed. It was a war, after all, and people got killed in wars, lots of people. Malcolm wasn't going to even consider that possibility. Being without Rose scared him too much to even contemplate it. He could wait. He would always wait for his Rose. *Damn her!*

⚏ Bibliography ⚏

Hosptial at War, by Zachary B. Friedenberg

And if I Perish – Frontline U.S. Army Nurses in World War II, by Evelyn M. Monahan and Rosemary Niedel-Greenlee

Angels of Mercy – the Army Nurses of World War II, by Betsy Kuhn

Bedpan Commando, by June Wandrey

Nurses Under Fire, by Brenda Jones

No time for Fear, by Diane Burke Fessler

Death Cheaters, by John Charles George

The World at War, H.P. Willmott, Robin Cross, Charles Messenger

The War – An Intimate History 1941 – 1945, by Geoffry C. Ward and Ken Burns
World War II Chronicle, ISBN 978-1-4127-1378-8

The Complete Guide to Fighters and Bombers of the World, by Francis Crosby

All American All the Way – the Combat History of the 88ᵗʰ Airborne Divison in World War II, by Phil Nordyke

Historic Baton Rouge – An Illustrated History, by Sylvia Frank Rodrique and Faye Phillips

Secrets of Beau Rivage – A novel of the mid 1930s, by Bob and Vel Evans

Pamphlet – *Flying Tigers, American Volunteer Group – Chinese Air Force*. I'm not sure who made up this pamphlet. It doesn't say anywhere inside it, but my Aunt Kay Wolf who was married to a Flying Tiger, gave it to me.

Days of the Ching Pao, by Malcolm Rosholt

Dog Sugar 8, by Malcolm Rosholt

The Flying Tigers, by John Toland

Flying Tigers, by Daniel Ford

The Maverick War – Chennault and the Flying Tigers, by Duane Schultz

World War II – The American Story 1939-1945, edited by Time –Life Books

The Stars and Stripes Story of WW II, by Robert Meyer Jr.

Citizen Soldiers, by Stephen Ambrose

A BURNISHED ROSE

Band of Brothers, by Stephen Ambrose

The Greatest Generation, by Tom Brokaw

The Good War - an oral history of world war II, by Studs Terke

The Battle of the Bulge - Hitler's last gamble in the West, by James Arnold

Across the Rhine - World War II, by Franklin M. Davis Jr. and the editors of Time-Life Books

Spearheading with the Third Armored Division, written in 1945 by an unknown author

Atlas of World War II, by David Jordan and Andrew Wiest

They Call it Purple Heart Valley – A Combat Chronicle of the War in Italy, by Margaret Bourke-White

Beautiful Crescent - A history of New Orleans, by Joan Garvey and Mary Lou Widmer

Wisconsin Medicine – Historical Perspectives, edited by Ronald Number and Judith Leavitt

Once Upon an Time When We Were Colored, by Clifton Taulbert

Rural Wisconsin – Time Honored Values of the Midwest, by Jerry Apps

Once They Were Eagles – Men of the Black Sheep Squadron, by Frank E. Walton

Voices of the Wisconsin Past – Women Remember the War, 1941-1945

U.S. Air Force – a complete history, published by Hugh Lauter Levin Assoc. inc

Picture History of the 20ᵗʰ Century, by Time Wood and RJ Unstead

Algeria, by Zurlo Tony

Algeria, by Falag Kagda and Zawiah Abdul Latif

Morocco, by Martin Hintz

Atlas of the World, eight addition - National Geographic

Romeo and Juliet, Oxford University Press, edited by Roma Gill

Conversations with God, by Neale Donald Walsch

Glossary

Louisiana Creole

Bel – beautiful

Cheri – sweetheart

Fonmiy - family

Gran-mer – grandmother

Konpronn - understand

Kouiyon - imbecile

Laime - love

Mamzel – lady

Mardi Gras – fat Tuesday

Misyeu – Mr.

Mo - I or my

Moman - mother

Mon Dur - my God

Orevoia - goodbye

Twa lonnens - two years

Tres byen - very good

French

Cher - dear

Comment allez-vous? - How are you?

Dieu vous bénisse, ma fille - God bless you, my daughter /girl

Enchanté - pleased to meet you

Et voici est Ginny *et* Miss Edna Dubay, but *Mad-dame préfere* Madam E. - And this is Ginny and Miss Edna Dubay, but Madam prefers Madam E.

Et cette est - And this is…

Formidable - terrific

"*Je peux vous présenter* Bridget, *et* May, Jolene, Ruth *et* Tess. Sadie *et la fille*, Millie are *là-bas*" - I would like to introduce Bridget, and May, Jolene, Ruth and Tess. Sadie and her daughter Millie are over there

Madame - Mrs.

Mon ami - my friend

Mon Dieu - my God

Mon marié - my husband

Monsieur - Mr.

No marié - no husband

Seulement une a l à fois - Only one at a time

Très bon - very good

Une minute - one minute

Voulez-vous des neafs frais, cher? - Want fresh eggs, my dear?

Votre marié? - Your husband?

"Vous allez vous marier bientôt. Je suis sûre. - You are getting married soon, I am sure.

Japanese

Fei-her - flying tiger

◩ About the Author ◩

Christine is a writer, reader, author, editor, book designer and publisher. She enjoys writing and helping others publish the book of their dreams through her publishing company: CKBooks Publishing. She started writing stories in college (a while ago!) and hasn't stopped since. Her first book: *Rosebloom*, won a national IPPY award in 2008 for historical fiction, her 2014 book: *Will the Real Carolyn Keene Please Stand Up* was a finalist for a Midwest Book Award for historical fiction, and her 2016 middle grade book: *Intrigue in Istanbul: An Agnes Kelly Mystery Advernture* won a Moonbeam Children's Book Award. Christine's publishing company is at ckbookspublishing.com. Her personal blog is at ckbooksblog.wordpress.com. You can see all her books at christinekelenybooks.com. This is also where you can sign up for her Readers Group.

Christine lives with her husband and pets in Wisconsin.

If you enjoyed this story, please leave a review on our favorite website. As an independent author, reviews are very helpful to Christine and she would like to know what you think.

The third and final book in the Rose Series is *Rose From the Ashes* and follows Rose's rocky return to civilian life.